DESIROUS

K.M. SCOTT

DESIROUS

Somebody's got it out for Kat Truesdale, and to her surprise, it isn't her one-time nemesis Alex March. Not that their brief romance hasn't crashed and burned, just like she worried it would.

There are two types of people in this world: the ones like Alex, who get all they want, and the ones like Kat, who always seem to have to fight for every last thing they need.

Kat knew it could never work with someone like him, but she secretly hoped this time would be different.

Alex loved his life and being single, but something about Kat Truesdale made him want to try being a one-woman man for once. Now that their relationship has gone to hell, he feels like something's changed in his life.

Gone is the desire to just be the player he used to be, but can he win her back now that she's sworn she never wants to see him again?

Desirous is a work of fiction. Names, characters, places, and events are the products of the author's imagination. Any resemblance to events, locations, or persons, living or dead, is coincidental.

Published in the United States

ISBN: 978-1-955335-17-1

CHAPTER ONE

lex

The entire March and Jackson clan is here at my grandmother's for one of our family get-togethers to celebrate something or another. Knowing these people, it's a party to commemorate the wind blowing. My family can't pass up a chance to gather all of us up at this house and eat and drink like we aren't sure we're going to make it to tomorrow.

Normally, I don't mind these impromptu events, but today, the last thing I want to do is hang out with my family and have to make conversation with them. So I've found myself a nice spot down near the water where I hope no one will bother me.

That's a pipe dream, of course. None of these

people could leave someone alone if they had a gun held to their head. It's just not in their nature.

Closing my eyes, I let the sun warm my face as I listen to the gentle sound of the water lapping against the sand. I'll have to move my spot in a little while, but until then, I'm enjoying nature alone, the way I want to be today.

I hear them all laughing and toasting something or another. Liam and Mia probably just walked in. Everyone gets very excited when a star shows up to the party.

Not that I blame them. She's a big deal. Liam hit the motherlode when he got together with her. Beauty, money, fame—she's got everything going for her. He's a lucky guy.

Cash and Cade are too. Their girlfriends are both beautiful and sweet and crazy about them. I'm happy they found the ones they're meant to be with for a lifetime.

Until recently, that's all their happiness meant to me. It was a good for them kind of thing. I didn't want that for my life, but hey, if they wanted to settle down, who was I to say they shouldn't? I planned on having to wear a tux a few times in the near future and that was it.

And then I met Kat, and everything changed.

I don't even know when it happened. Somewhere between her expressing her loathing for me at the beginning of the reality show and the moment I stood there in the parking lot outside the studio watching her drive away after telling me she hated me and never wanted to see me again, I fell for her.

I push that thought down, hidden deep inside me so I don't have to think about it. I didn't fall for her. That's ridiculous. I'm a guy who plans to spend the rest of his life enjoying it, and that doesn't include falling in love with some woman whose go-to emotion seems to be misery.

So she hates me. Welcome to the club. I can name at least ten women who said they hated me at some point of another, usually once they wanted things to get more serious and I headed toward the door.

Go ahead, hate me. What does it matter?

My shoulders slowly inch up toward my ears as I think about Kat, so I force them down and tilt my head left and then right to crack my neck. Talk about stress. That woman comes with a boatload of it. Even when she's nowhere nearby, I can't help but be a stressed-out mess merely thinking about her.

If this is what it's like when you care about someone, the world can keep it. I haven't had a moment's happiness since she drove away. Why would anyone willingly want to put themselves through this for anyone?

I sense someone coming up behind my chair to interrupt my perfectly relaxing time and open my eyes to see Cade standing next to me. He has a look of intention in his eyes, like he's been sent on a mission. Likely by my mother.

"Did you come to sit quietly and enjoy the sound of the water as it rolls in?" I ask, hoping he's like he used to be and understands the concept of not wanting to talk.

"No. I came to see why you're sitting down here like some curmudgeonly old man who doesn't want to socialize with anyone he's related to," he says, answering my question with the only words I didn't want to hear.

I twist my face into a hard grimace and pray to God he understands that means go away. But he doesn't. Instead, he plops down onto the sand next to me and draws his knees up like he's getting ready for some long chat between us.

The chairs that usually accompany mine aren't here for a reason. You'd think my family could read the room. Or the beach, as it were.

My best friend never used to be so unwilling or unable to see when I wasn't in the mood to talk. That's what made him such an incredible friend. Cade could tell just by my expression if he should back off and give me some space, but ever since he got together with Hailey, it's like he completely lost all ability to understand me.

That's what women do for you.

"So are you going to tell me what the hell is wrong,

or do I have to bring out the big guns?" he asks with a smile.

I narrow my eyes in disgust and let my gaze roll over his arms. "Big guns? I'm not sure I'd call what you're packing the big guns."

Even though I know what he means when he says that, I can't help but bust his balls a little after he intentionally interrupted my time alone down here. That's what you get for ignoring the bro code, dude.

I get a frown for my teasing and then an eyeroll. "I'm talking about your mother, shithead. She's all concerned up there on the porch and wanted to come down to see if you're okay. I told her I'd do it since I knew you wouldn't want to tell your mother what the hell is wrong."

As if that helps me any.

"I don't want to tell you either, so feel free to go back to hanging out with your girlfriend and all the other happy March and Jackson people. I'll be fine down here."

Once more, I close my eyes to enjoy the sounds of nature around me, but this time it's also to give Cade the clearest sign that there's nothing to talk about with me. He doesn't say anything for a long time, so I assume he came around to remembering that we don't need to discuss about what's bothering us like the rest of our family does.

And then he disappoints me by opening his mouth.

"Alex, what the hell is wrong with you? Dude,

you're sitting down here sulking like Wilder, for fuck's sake."

That makes me open my eyes, and I turn to give a look that could kill for his mention of the one cousin we both can't stand. "First you threaten me with the big guns, and now you go low? That's shitty, man. Wilder? Come on. Really?"

A slow smile lights up Cade's expression. "I needed something to get your attention, so I figured I'd hit you with that and see how you reacted. At least I know you haven't completely changed your personality and now you actually like that asshole."

"Nobody likes Wilder, dude. Well, Kane and Abbi do, but even Liam can't stand his bullshit. The guy is nothing but trauma drama and hassle."

Cade levels his gaze on my face and gives me the raised eyebrow look like I'm missing something big. "And you're any less drama sitting down here all by yourself knowing everyone will want to know what's going on with you? Come on, Alex. You had to know they weren't going to let you hang out here in peace. This is the March family we're talking about."

Now it's my turn to roll my eyes. Drama. Like I want any of them to bother me. Fucking drama would be telling everyone how I feel and then expecting them to feel bad like Wilder does all the time.

"All I wanted was some peace and quiet. I'm here, aren't I? I didn't bail on the family get-together, even though all I wanted to do was stay home and be alone.

But no, I dragged my ass here, just like they all want, so why can't I just be left alone to enjoy the water and the sun? Is it too much to ask this family? When the hell have I ever bothered any of them? I live and let live. Do I get all up in anyone's business when they don't want to talk? Nope, not me. I just let them be. It's a damn shame I can't get the same consideration in return."

But nothing I say makes Cade walk away, unfortunately.

"So what, now you're thinking the people in our family suddenly aren't the nosy bastards they always are, Don Quixote? Where oh where can I find a windmill for you?" he says with a healthy dose of sarcasm in his voice.

"It isn't quixotic to want a single day when I don't have to talk to anyone, even though I came to this thing today."

He laughs at my need to tilt at that windmill. "You know, Mrs. Mapleby would be so impressed with our use of that word right now. I feel like I'm channeling eighth grade vocab class today."

The memory of the two of us causing trouble for that poor old lady every day of the school year makes me smile. We used to be a pair of jackasses back then.

"Remember her mumbling under her breath every time one of us said anything? What did she call us?"

Cade grins from ear to ear. "The Trouble Twins. She had no idea what we were capable of."

"Used to be capable of," I say in a low voice.

"Is that what this whole moping around shit is about? I know you and I don't hang out as much as we used to, but we still get together."

Of course, he misunderstood what I meant. Everyone thinks I'm unhappy because Cade, Cash, and Liam are all with someone they love and I'm still single. As far as I can tell, love isn't all that it's cracked up to be, so I don't know why anyone's wishing it on me.

The truth is I'm more disgusted with myself and what I don't seem to be able to do anymore. There was a time when I could go out at night and pick up women with no problem. We'd go back to my place, enjoy ourselves, and then part ways, everyone happy and content with the good time we gave one another.

Now I'm some sad mess who can't stop thinking about one woman, despite the fact that I've had ample opportunities to go out and find women since Kat and I slept together.

"This doesn't have anything to do with you, Cade," I say as I stare straight ahead at the blue water in front of me. "I don't begrudge you your happiness with Hailey. I know the rest of you think I do or I have some resentment about everyone finding someone, but that's not it at all."

"Then what is it? You seemed happy as a clam that night when you came to see me at Club X. I know you hooked up with those two women, which can't be the reason you're unhappy because come on, a threesome never fails to make you happy. So what the hell is wrong?"

I wish all it would take is a threesome to make me happy again. Hell, I'd do that in a heartbeat if it meant I'd be myself and not this miserable mess I've become.

Then again, I probably wouldn't because neither of the women would be Kat. There goes that great plan.

"I really don't want to talk about it, Cade. You know me better than anyone else in the world, so I need you to see that talking isn't what I need right now."

Thankfully, that gets through to him, and he stands up to leave me alone. "I get it. Okay. If and when you want to talk, I'm always around, Alex. For what it's worth, nobody is trying to get up in your business. It's just that we aren't used to seeing you like this."

"I'll be fine. I just need to be alone for a little while."

"Is this about that show?"

Turning my head, I give him a death stare and hope he gets it now. He lifts his hands like he's surrendering and begins to back away.

"Okay, forget I asked. I'm going to go now. Let me know when you want to talk again, okay?"

I force a smile and when he walks away toward the house, I return my focus to the water in front of me slowly creeping closer. Soon my feet will be covered, but maybe I'll stay here and let myself get wet. It's not like I have anywhere to go after this.

Just home. Alone.

But not five minutes later, I hear someone walking down the yard toward me. That's the problem with this family. There's no goddamned respect for anyone's wishes. I wonder if smaller families come with this much hassle.

"Alex, honey, won't you come up and join us? Your Aunt Abbi brought a peach cobbler, and I know that's one of your favorites. She'd love it if you'd come up and have some."

I don't want to unload on my mother, but I swear it's taking every ounce of strength I possess to not bark at her that I just want to be left the fuck alone. How is that so difficult to understand?

Her dark eyes so like mine are filled with such hope that I can't snap at her, but I don't want to join them all for peach cobbler. I don't know what to say to make them see I just want to be left alone.

"Mom, thanks, but not now. Maybe later," I say with a smile pasted onto my face in the hopes that she'll take that and be happy.

"Are you sure? She worked really hard on it. It would mean the world to her if you came up and had some."

My façade of geniality fades a little as I say, "And it would mean the world to me if everyone would leave me alone."

That's all it takes to make my mother frown and sadness fill her eyes. "Okay. Do you think you'll come up anytime today?"

I let out a heavy sigh, already done with all these attempts at making me join in the family fun. "I don't know, Mom. I'm okay, so you don't have to worry. I just don't want to socialize today."

"Okay."

She leaves, but I see the beginning of sulking come over her, which means my father will be down here in about a minute after he sees her pouty face. It never fails. He always feels like he has to ride in on his white horse when her feelings are hurt. I didn't mean to upset her, but it won't matter.

Down he'll come.

And just like clockwork, less than a minute later, my father appears at my side like some disgruntled hero ready to make things right. Except there's nothing he can do for me, so I wish he'd go back up to the porch and make my mother feel better.

"Alex, what's going on? Your mother says you don't want to come up for some of your aunt's peach cobbler. I thought you loved that every time she made it."

I want to bark at him, but I don't, even as the idea occurs to me that he would never pull this shit on Cash. My brother gets to be silent because it's his way. Because everyone's used to me being happy-go-lucky, I'm not allowed a single day of solitude.

His blue eyes gaze down at me with more than a little curiosity. I've seen that look before with him, usually when something happens at the restaurant.

But we aren't there, and I don't have any obligation to say another word since I'm not his employee right now. I'm just his son.

Still, I know if I don't say something, he'll end up leaving and someone else will come down. They'll probably send Liam down next. Or maybe Stefan, but I doubt that. They might suggest it, but I can see my uncle telling them a hearty fuck no. Out of all of my family, he gets it when someone doesn't want to talk. I've always gotten the vibe that he could never come to another one of these March and Jackson family get-togethers and be completely happy about it.

Worst would be if they sent Kane down. He's generally more sullen than anyone else, and that would just put me in an even more unpleasant mood. Misery certainly would love company then.

"Dad, maybe later, okay? Right now, I just want to be alone. That's it. I'm not asking for anything that costs a thing. Really. I just want to be left alone for a little while."

"Does this have anything to do with a girl?" he asks with all the earnestness of a priest.

That's it. I can't handle this today. I need to get the hell away from all these goddamned questions before I flip out.

Jumping up out of my chair, I shake my head as I

try to hold back the anger. "First of all, Dad, I'm twenty-five. If I'm hanging out with girls, I've got much bigger problems than what's really on my mind. Second of all, I asked every one of you who came down here to just let me be, and every one of you reacted to that simple request with more goddamned questions. What is it with this family?"

I storm away before he can answer that question since I have no real interest in hearing his explanation. By the time I reach the porch, I see my mother's face light up with pure happiness as she assumes I've finally given in and decided to be sociable.

"Oh, honey, I'm glad you chose to come up and be with us," she says as I hit the first step up to the porch.

"I didn't. I just couldn't get any damn peace and quiet with everyone doing their best impression of the intrusive conga line down to me on the beach, so I'm going inside. Please don't come talk to me or follow me. In fact, I'd appreciate it if you all would just leave me the hell alone!"

The entire family stares at me with wide eyes full of shock. I guess I won't be thought of as the happy-go-lucky one in the March and Jackson clan anymore.

CHAPTER TWO

lex

By the time I reach my favorite bedroom in my grandmother's house, I'm a strange combination of angry and guilty. I didn't want to unload on all of them like that. I told them exactly what I wanted, and still they refused to do as I asked.

Then again, they are used to me being pretty easygoing all the time. They probably have no idea how to react to how I'm acting today.

I don't want to think about more people I've pissed off. It was bad enough to know Kat thinks I'm a selfish bastard. Now I guess my family thinks the same.

Great.

Looking around the room, I smile at how little it's

changed since I used to sleep here as a little boy. The same blue curtains my grandmother bought when I first began staying over when I was only five. The same pale blue bedspread and blue sheets. I guess my grandmother assumed since we were boys she should make everything that color.

Back then, she'd take Cade and me for weekends, and I swear she'd barely see us from sunup to sundown. We'd have breakfast with her and then race out the back door to play outside. We'd swim and build sandcastles and bury one another in the sand up to our chins. Then we'd come in for lunch before hurrying outside for another few hours until dinner. By the time bedtime came, she barely had enough time to tell us to take a bath and brush our teeth before we collapsed into our beds.

Those were good days.

I sit down on the bed that seems so much smaller now and look at the pictures that have been hanging on the wall since we were boys. A Bucs poster back before they became a team anyone feared hangs on the wall near the window, and a Dolphins one for Cade hangs on the other side of the window.

A picture of the two of us when we were no more than seven sits in a gold frame next to the TV on the dresser. I can't help but smile as the memory of that day comes flooding back to me. Cade got stung by a jellyfish, and because I had heard that you should urinate on where it got you, I pissed all over his calf.

We were little boys, so pissing and whipping our junk out was second nature. Alexandria was mortified and hurried him inside, ordering him to get into the shower immediately. It turned out the piss did nothing to help.

But we had so much fun that day that she took a picture of us smiling like it was the best day of our lives.

"You know, I never spanked any of you grandchildren because that's not what grandmothers do, but I came close that day with you, Alex."

I look over toward the door to see my grandmother standing there smiling at me. "I thought I was always your favorite."

She nods and walks over to sit down next to me on the bed. "You are. Between you and me, I think you might be your mother's favorite too. Don't tell Cash I said that. He's got your father's approval, though, so he'll be fine."

With a chuckle, I smile at her assessment of who's the favorite for our parents. I know my mother has always had a special place in her heart for me. She used to tell me Cash was her miracle baby since she didn't think she would ever be able to have children, but I was nothing short of incredible since I was her second miracle.

"I didn't mean to snap at her like that," I quietly admit.

My grandmother shrugs and smooths her white

hair off her forehead. "Don't worry. Your mother will be fine. She's tougher than she looks. Your father tends to baby her, which don't get me wrong isn't a bad thing. He could be like your grandfather. That would be bad."

"I just wanted to be left alone."

She smiles and shakes her head. "I've seen this condition many times in my life. It's a woman, isn't it?"

I wave away her suggestion that it could be a woman making me act like this. "Me? Have women problems? Please. I leave that kind of stuff for Cash and Liam. They're the ones who always have women problems."

"Don't lie to me, Alexander March. I can see it as clear as day written all over your face," she says, wagging her finger as she chastises me.

Is it that obvious? No wonder everyone kept insisting on trying to get me to talk.

"It's not like that. At least, it's not what you think," I say, trying to hedge my way out of talking about my woman problems with my grandmother, of all people.

She lets out a heavy sigh and shakes her head. "You've always had it very easy, honey. I wondered when that would run out and you'd have to deal with things like your brother and cousins have had to all their lives."

Yet another person in the world who thinks my life has been one huge cakewalk.

Turning to face her, I ask, "Why is it that everyone

thinks I've had it so easy all my life? I had to go to school to be a chef. It's not like that was handed to me. Yes, I work in the restaurant my father and uncle own, but I had to prove myself to all those people in the kitchen, and trust me, they weren't willing to give me an inch of leeway exactly because of who I'm related to."

My grandmother gives me one of those smiles that says I've completely misunderstood what she meant. Patting my arm, she sighs again.

"Oh, Alex, this has nothing to do with your job. Everyone knows how hard you work and how much of your time and energy you've given to make CK the best restaurant in town. This has to do with you."

Now I'm utterly confused. What is she talking about?

"What about me?"

Her dark eyes filled with kindness look into mine as she explains, "You were such a handsome child, and even when your brother and your cousins went through their awkward stages, you never did. I used to joke with your parents that you were the chosen one with how easily things came to you. Looks, personality, confidence—you never lacked in any of those areas. On top of that, you were smart and charming, two traits others have to work to perfect and often never do. In many ways, I was waiting with more than a little apprehension for this day to come because I wasn't sure how you'd handle it."

Lowering my gaze to the floor, I say, "You mean the day I became miserable? Because that's how I feel. Miserable. I've never felt like this, and I don't know how to fix myself or the situation causing me to feel this way."

"That tells me it must be a woman because nothing else would make you so unhappy."

I blow the air out of my lungs and let my shoulders sag. "Okay, fine. It's a woman. I don't know why I can't just forget her. It's not like we were together forever, and it's not like we were good together. I mean, the woman started off knowing me by saying she couldn't stand me."

For some reason, my grandmother finds that amusing. With a laugh, she says, "And yet you charmed her into falling for you, just like with all the others."

I wouldn't say that's how it went. As far as I'm concerned, I used very little charm with Kat. If anything, I think her attitude toward me simply thawed enough to see I wasn't the monster she had made me out to be. After that, all we had in common simply made getting together natural.

"Unfortunately, Grandma, my charm isn't going to solve this problem. She hates me. She thinks I'm a selfish bastard who she never wants to see again."

Alexandria March waves away that idea like it's nothing she's terribly worried about. Lucky her. She has no idea how sure Kat sounded in the studio parking lot last week.

"You're just like me, Alex. It's no coincidence that we have nearly identical names. No man could ever tell me no, just like women love to be around you. It's charisma. People want to like you. Use that to your advantage like you always have. You'll see. It'll work."

Again, I let out a heavy sigh, wishing she was right. "Not this time. This one is immune to my charms. I've tried to call her. I tried texting. She won't answer."

Suddenly, my grandmother changes right before my eyes, and I see judgment coming from her. "Did you do something you shouldn't be forgiven for, Alex?"

As much as I'd love to be able to answer unequivocally no, that's not the truth. I've never been able to lie to my grandmother, though, so I might as well just tell her what I did and get it over with.

"I didn't mean to hurt her. Honest. The producers of that reality show accused her of poisoning someone, and I knew she didn't do that, so I told them so. I could have done more to convince them, and that's why she hates me because they threw her off the show, and now she has no chance of winning the million-dollar prize."

"Did you do that because you want to win?"

The matriarch of my family never has been the type to pull any punches. I guess expecting her to go easy on me because I'm her favorite grandson was too much to ask this time.

"I do want to win that money because I would love to have my own restaurant and not have to wait for my father and Kane to retire, but mostly, I didn't say more because if I had told the producers how I knew she couldn't have been the one to poison the food, we both would have been thrown off the show."

"Why is that?"

Looking away so I don't have to meet her gaze when I admit I was Kat's alibi because we were in bed together all night, I say, "Because in the contract we signed, there's a clause that says there is to be no fraternizing among contestants. How I know she didn't poison anyone is the textbook definition of fraternizing."

"Oh. I see. You know, if I was this woman, I'd be angry with you too. That said, I still believe you can fix this. Go to her. Tell her how you feel. Just be honest with her."

As images of Kat throwing a cast iron frying pan at me flash through my brain, I shake my head. "It isn't that easy, Grandma."

She wraps her arms around me and pulls me close for a hug. In my ear, she whispers, "Yes, it is, honey. Never forget that. When you find what you love, then everything falls into place. It happened with you when you knew you wanted to be a chef, and it will happen with this woman, if you truly care for her."

As she gets up to leave, all I can think is I wish it was that easy.

"Now quit sulking and come down and eat some of your aunt's peach cobbler. You know how everyone gets if the family chef won't eat something they made. I'll have to hear about it until the day I die."

"Okay, Grandma. I'll be down in a few."

"Good. And then when you're done making Abbi happy, you can leave to go make amends with this woman so you don't have to stay here and explain to your parents and everyone else what's wrong. You know how nosy everyone in this family can be."

I can't help but smile as she walks out of the room. The nosiness starts with the head of the family, and she knows it.

Maybe she's right. Maybe it won't be impossible to convince Kat that I'm sorry. Maybe she's already cooled down enough to forgive me.

CHAPTER THREE

at

THIS BED MIGHT BE WHERE I SPEND THE REST OF MY life. It's comfortable, the sheets smell like that flowery fabric softener Sadie loves to use on the wash, and there's no chance of getting hurt here. Yes, this could be the place where I live out the rest of my days.

I'll have to arrange for food and drink to come to me, but I bet Sadie will take pity on me for a few days. After that, I may have to get out of bed, but only long enough to run to the kitchen and grab some sustenance.

And to go to the bathroom. That's definitely something I'll need to get out of bed for. I'm depressed, but that doesn't mean I'm so far gone that I don't care about cleanliness.

My roommate appears in the doorway and tilts her head like she's getting ready to talk to a small child. I must really look pathetic if she's acting that way after only a few days of my hiding out in here.

"Kat, do you want to get up and maybe come out to the couch? We could talk," she says in a sweet voice.

I shake my head. "I'm good right here. These covers have accepted me as one of them, so I can't leave now."

"You still have your sense of humor. That's good, at least."

Pulling the sheet down to expose my mouth, I say, "I've got a joke for you. Want to hear it?"

Sadie's face lights up. "Sure!"

"There was this woman who thought she could turn her life around. She tried out for this reality show and believed she had a chance. But that was a lie she told herself. Now she has no chance of winning the million-dollar prize, and why? Because the man she slept with and was really believing she had something special with sold her out the first chance he got. Now the woman has to go back to work humiliated, and her boss will no doubt take full advantage of that and make her life a living hell. Ha-ha! Hysterical, right?"

My friend frowns. I guess my joke wasn't funny

after all. Well, at least I'm not the only one who understands how bad things are.

"Do you want to talk about it?"

Again, I shake my head. "If I say much more, I'll start crying again, and I'm so damn tired of crying. I'd like to move out of the sadness stage and move into the one where I'm pissed and taking it out on the people who deserve it. Well, the one person who deserves it. Alex Freaking March."

Sadie chuckles. "You know, you can say fuck here. It's not like I can't handle it."

I pat the bed around my body. "The covers have delicate sensibilities. Probably from the fabric softener you used on them the last time you washed for me. Thanks for that, by the way. I didn't realize how important that would turn out to be until the past few days."

"You're welcome. You sure you don't want to come out into the living room and hang out while I eat some dinner? I have more than enough for both of us."

I appreciate Sadie's attempts to bring me out of my darkness, but it's no use. This is where I belong. At least until I have to go to work tomorrow.

She begins to say something, but my phone ringing interrupts her. Rolling over, I grab it off the nightstand and glance at the screen.

Fucking Alex March.

He's called me no less than five times in the past couple days. Less than a deranged stalker but definitely more than I would have expected from someone like him.

I hold the phone up to show Sadie. "He thinks he can just keep calling and that will make everything all better."

"Have you spoken to him at all?" she asks, hinting that she thinks I should.

Dropping the phone onto the bed, I watch as it continues to ring. "No. Not since our final scene in the parking lot where I told him I hate him and never want to see him again. As far as I'm concerned, those are the last words I ever plan to say to him."

When he finally gives up this time, I feel less relieved than all the other times. I don't know why. It's not like I'm in danger of actually answering any of his calls. He can try until the end of time. I won't answer.

And then he calls again not a minute later, and I stare at my phone like it's my enemy. "You'd think he'd get the hint."

"He sounds pretty insistent. Some people might think that's a good thing."

I shoot Sadie a nasty look for being such a nice person. Alex March doesn't deserve nice. "He's probably used to getting people to do whatever he wants by whatever means necessary. He wants to charm me, but because I won't answer his calls, he plans on trying to wear me down until I give in."

"You aren't ever going to speak to him again?"

Sadie and I have completely opposite ways of

dealing with heartbreak. She eats a ton of ice cream, talks out her feelings until she's better, and never denies anyone the chance to explain themselves. I think it's madness, but it works for her.

I, on the other hand, crawl into my fluffy and flowery-smelling cave and don't come out until I'm sure I won't cry or until I have to because my rent doesn't pay itself. I don't eat. I don't want to talk to the person who broke my heart. I just stay in bed.

"There's nothing he could say that I need to hear."

My phone falls silent, and I stuff it under the pillow to hide it away from my sight. Sadie points at it and grimaces. "Is that you pretending you're smothering him?"

I hadn't thought of that. Maybe she does have a dark side after all.

"No. That's me ignoring him. Forever."

After giving me sympathetic eyes that make me feel like some kind of sad thing, she says, "I'm going to eat dinner. Let me know if you're interested in having any. I got a turkey club from that place we used to go to all the time."

"The place that failed the health inspection?" I ask in horror. "What made you go back there?"

Always giving people a second chance. I swear it's going to get her hurt someday. At the very least it might get her food poisoning tonight.

"It's under new ownership, so I thought I'd give it

a try. The club looks good. Sure you don't want some?"

I give her a nod and leave her to the potential food poisoning case she's likely to get from mayonnaise that's been out too long in that skeevy diner's kitchen.

Closing my eyes, I try not to focus on the possibility that Sadie will be spending the entire night worshipping the porcelain goddess. Better to think about how miserable Alex feels knowing there's at least one person in this world who won't let him charm his way out of the mess he made. I hope he feels like shit. It's the least he could do since I've felt that way from the moment I realized he wasn't going to stand up for me with Chef on Chef's producers.

The moment the tears start welling in my eyes, I shake my head to will them away. No more tears for that jackass. I will not give him any more. He doesn't deserve them.

I curl up into a ball under my nice, safe covers and hope to drift off to sleep. At least then I won't be thinking about how terrible my life is. The police haven't come to take me away for attempted murder, so I guess that's something good. They'll probably show up eventually, though.

My mind drifts back to the night Alex and I spent together, and for a few sweet moments, I remember how incredible it felt to be with him. For the first time in my life, I was the kind of woman I always dreamed of being. I don't want to give him any credit for that, but he brought that out in me.

And then he betrayed me the first chance he could get.

God, I don't want to think about him or what happened anymore. If I could just fall asleep, I wouldn't have to feel or remember anything. Before I can drift off, though, I hear someone knocking at the front door. Maybe Sadie already called the ambulance to take her to the hospital to get her stomach pumped. I knew that sandwich wouldn't be okay.

Then a few seconds later, I hear her open it and say the one name I didn't expect her to say. "Oh. Hi, Alex."

Did he actually come here to try to talk to me? I underestimated him. I thought he'd give up trying when I didn't answer his nearly ten phone calls. Then it dawns on me. Of course, he came here. Charm works so much better in person.

Well, he can forget that because I'm not getting out of this bed.

"Is Kat here?" he asks in a voice that sounds like the one he used when he attempted to make me see he wasn't a total snake that day he betrayed me.

"She doesn't want to see you. I'm sorry," Sadie says, far too nicely, in my opinion.

Don't be pleasant to him! He doesn't deserve it. Trust me.

"I just want to talk to her. I tried calling a bunch of

times, but she won't answer my calls. Can you please tell her I'm here?"

Damn, he really does sound sad. Maybe I should at least yell out that I don't want to see him. At least that will give him the clue that I'll never answer his calls so he can stop trying.

No! Do not fall for that sad sack man voice. Every male on the planet has that voice they use when they know they've fucked up, and it works on far too many women. He feels bad? Good. He should feel bad. I feel like shit, so he should too.

"I heard what you did, Alex. I thought you were a better person than that," Sadie says in a tone that's downright disapproving.

Yes, girl! That's the way to do it! Don't let him stand there and give you those puppy dog eyes and that pathetic voice to make you think he's torn up about things. Tell him he's a bastard.

"I didn't mean to fuck up like I did. I know I messed everything up, but I want to make amends."

The conversation falls silent, and I inch over on the bed to get a better chance of hearing what they're saying. Is she whispering something to him? Or is she giving him her best look of disappointment? I've seen that expression once or twice. Coming from someone as sweet as Sadie, it's brutal.

"Well, she doesn't want to talk to you. I know that."

"Will you tell her I came by and I want to talk to her? Please?"

Oh, that was a good touch. Please? I half expected him to follow up with a pretty please. I can see his face now. Those brown eyes of his the color of milk chocolate staring into hers with all the sincerity he can muster in his attempt to get her to do what he wants. I've seen that look before. That night we spent together. It wasn't so much pleading as it was seductive, but I bet it works on every woman he meets.

It worked on me. God, I'm such a fool!

I hear the door close and scurry across the bed to where I was before so Sadie doesn't see I was making an effort to listen. I don't want her to think I cared because I don't.

She appears in the doorway looking glum. He got to her. I knew it! I knew she'd buy his pathetic act.

"Hey, did you hear any of that?" she asks, likely knowing the answer already before I say a word.

"Some," I lie, not wanting to look like I care.

"I think he feels really bad, Kat. He looked sad."

Rolling my eyes, I don't try to hide my disgust at how easily fooled she can be. "He looked the way he needed to look to convince you that he felt bad about being a dick."

"Whatever, but I think he's sorry."

I pull the covers up over my head and mumble, "I think you're too nice."

"Maybe, but that doesn't change the fact that I think he really cares for you and hates that he messed up."

I don't bother to respond to that craziness. Sadie's always too nice. It's the reason she always ends up with her heart in pieces when relationships end. Then again, here I am in the same situation, and no one could ever accuse me of being too nice.

So much for walls protecting a girl, huh?

CHAPTER FOUR

lex

After I turn off my car, I check my phone to see if Kat's called or texted back. My heart sinks as I see nothing from her. Not a single missed call or text.

I've got it all planned out for this morning. After my unsuccessful visit to Kat's apartment last night, proof that my grandmother was wrong, sadly, I lay in bed staring up at the ceiling half the night trying to find a way to fix things since clearly talking to Kat isn't going to be enough.

Well, if bigger gestures are necessary, so be it. I can't let her go on thinking that I sold her out just to have a chance at that million dollars. Yes, I want to win, but even more, I need her to see I'm not the selfish son of a bitch she thinks I am.

At least, I don't want to be that with her.

Taking a deep breath, I head into the studio for the first day of taping for the reality show. I'm here early so I can talk to Maria and Shane, and as soon as I walk on the set, I see them on the other side of the room talking to one another.

I know what very well may happen when I do this, but I don't care. Some things are more important than money. Some people are too.

"Hi, Maria, Shane. If you have a few minutes, I'd like to talk to you," I start off, making sure I don't sound contrite or ashamed.

I'm not. What I have to say is the truth, and if they react the way they should, I'll accept it as my just punishment for breaking their rules.

"Alex, you look great! You must have gotten good sleep in preparation for today," Maria says in her usual enthusiastic way.

"Not really, but you know, coffee. It's a magic drink."

Shane smiles, as if I said something funny or clever. "It is that for sure. You're here early this morning. Wanted to get a jump on the day? It's going to be exciting, so no one would blame you."

The two of them grin at me while I wonder if they get paid by the word. Nothing is ever simply said by either one of them. They take the idea of using as few words as possible and turn it on its head every chance they get.

"So, I wanted to talk to you about what happened last week with Kat."

Before I can continue, Shane steps toward me and wraps his arm around my shoulders. "We don't blame you, Alex, if that's what you're thinking. In fact, Maria and I were just talking about you and how to move forward."

I force myself to smile as I subtly twist out of his odd guy embrace. "I wasn't thinking that, but I did want to tell you something. Kat couldn't have done anything to that dish. You said security saw someone here the night before, but that couldn't have been her."

Just as I get to the point where I'm ready to admit I broke a central rule in the contract, Maria says, "I know you want to believe in people. I saw that the first time we met at CK, but Murphy's need to have his stomach pumped is proof that she did it. I hate to admit it too because I liked her, but it is what it is."

How terribly fucking Zen of Maria to distill the whole issue down to those five empty words.

Shaking my head at how dense this woman can be, I continue to defend Kat and admit my guilt. "No, it isn't proof that she did anything. When we left that day, the dish was fine. Whoever came here that night to tamper with it couldn't have been Kat because she was at my place all night. She isn't the person who poisoned Murphy, and she shouldn't be punished for that. It's not fair, and she should be brought back on the show."

When I finish confessing what we did, I wait for the two producers to exact their punishment as they should. I broke the rules, and I deserve what I get.

Maria simply stares at me in shock for a long moment while Shane hums beside me like he's trying to decide the right words to let me know I'm off the show. There's no need for him to worry. I know what I did went against that clause in my contract. I don't care. I don't regret being with Kat either.

The only thing I regret is not being the kind of man I should have been when they accused her of poisoning Murphy.

Once more, Shane gives me a man hug with his arm around my shoulders and says, "Well, we appreciate your honesty, Alex. I think that's going to be one of the many reasons viewers love you on this show."

"Oh, yes!" Maria chimes in. "Viewers of shows like this love when contestants show their honesty and vulnerability."

What? Didn't they hear what I said? Maybe I need to make it clear what I did.

I twist out of Shane's hold again and confess my crime in the most basic way possible. "I don't think you're hearing me right. I was with Kat, as in she stayed at my place all night because we were together. That's fraternizing, and although I probably should have remembered that before anything happened between us, I can't go on without admitting it."

Finally, Shane seems to understand what I'm saying. He hums for a long moment before asking, "So are you and Kat a couple now?"

Since I'm trying to be honest here, I decide to admit the truth about that too. "No. She can't forgive me for not telling you the truth that day, but now that I have, at least I can know I did the right thing, even if it was after the fact."

I wait for the two of them to tell me to get my things and leave because I'm off the show. Instead, Maria's eyes open wide, and she gives me a big smile like I've done something good.

"I love this man's style! Don't you, Shane? Thank you for being honest, Alex, but that just makes us want you on the show more. I'm glad you got that off your chest. Now we can tell you what we were talking about when you walked over."

My mouth drops open in shock as I try to think of a way to get the truth through to her, but it's no use. She and Shane look at me like I'm the best thing they've ever seen, which makes no sense, but nothing they do seems to make sense to me.

"So here's what we came up with," Shane says, completely ignoring everything I just confessed to in the past few minutes. "You need a romantic storyline now that yours blew up last week, so we've decided you and Emma will share one. What do you think?"

I stand there trying to find any words that don't involve asking both of them if they're stupid, but since I can't locate any in my brain, I just nod. What is there to say? I came on this damn show to cook, and once more, these two people seem hell bent on focusing on anything but making goddamned food.

"We think viewers will really take to you and Emma!" Maria squeals. "Even more than you and Kat, so don't worry. Everything's going to work out great!"

So much for the people watching this show loving my honesty. I guess they'll have to settle for my pretending to like someone who isn't the woman I care about.

"I guess. Thanks."

I don't know what else to say, so as they huddle together happy as clams at their brilliant idea to pair me with yet another female on this show about anything but cooking, I make my way over to my station. Other contestants begin to come onto the set, and while I still have a few free moments, I check my phone to see if Kat's returned any of my calls or texts.

Nothing.

I sigh in frustration, wishing she'd give me just one chance to explain things to her. I even tried to do the right thing here today, and what was my reward? Having to pretend to be crazy about Emma.

At least she's not terrible. Kat seemed to like her. She was kind to her more than once, so that says something about Emma.

Stuffing my phone into my pants pocket, I look up to see her grinning from ear to ear as she talks to Shane and Maria. At least she seems pleased by the news that she has to playact like we're a couple.

Then a horrible thought occurs to me. If Kat watches this show, she'll have to see me with her. Fuck.

Maybe she won't watch it. It's highly likely that she won't since I'm sure she has nothing but bad feelings about it. And me, of course.

Then again, what if she watches to see if I get my ass handed to me in the competition? Then she'll be treated to my fake romance with Emma.

Fuck and more fuck.

Mired in misery, I don't see my new bogus love interest come over and stand next to me until she taps me on the shoulder. Turning to look at her, I see she's more than happy about the new arrangement.

With a big smile, she says, "Maria and Shane told me we're to be together. Isn't that great?"

I try to muster a smile in return, but it never gets to the point that it could convince anyone I'm happy. "Sure. I guess since we don't have to do much cooking on this show, we have to fill in the time with something."

Her smile fades, but she bounces back quickly and nudges my arm. "You're such a kidder. I love it! We're going to have so much fun, you know that? I bet they have us do things outside of this set too."

Great. A field trip with my pretend love interest. What more could a chef ask for on a reality cooking show? God, I wish I had followed my gut about this whole thing.

Then again, if I had, I wouldn't have gotten to know Kat, so maybe all this misery was worth it. Now if only I could make her see I'm not the selfish fuck she's so sure I am.

CHAPTER FIVE

at

THE TIME HAS COME FOR ME TO LEAVE MY BED. TOO bad because I seriously could see me spending the rest of my life here.

But until I find a way to make money from my bedroom and look like a trainwreck doing it, I'll have to go back to work. Sadie doesn't deserve to suffer for my bad choices, and the rent is due next week, so off to the restaurant I go.

First, though, I need to eat something and wash off the multi-day sleepfest I've been enjoying. I haven't had an appetite for almost four days. Maybe I've lost a few pounds. That would be the only good thing to come out of my depressive state.

Padding out to the kitchen in my bare feet, I hop up on one of the barstools at the counter and open the cabinet to grab a sleeve of saltines. I doubt I could stomach much more right now, but I need something if I'm going to work a shift this afternoon.

I set my phone down and see no new messages or calls. I guess he gave up. Four days isn't bad. I didn't expect more than a call or two, so Alex actually surprised me.

With a shake of my head, I try to push that out of my mind. He didn't surprise me, so what the hell am I thinking? I always knew he was a selfish bastard, and the first chance he got, he proved me right in spades.

As I chew on dry crackers, I mindlessly scroll through my phone and then to my messages to read all the texts he sent. It's stupid, really. Why should I read them again? They aren't going to change from the first time. It must be hunger. That's what's making me sentimental. I need to eat more food so that goes away.

I let his first text come up, and my eyes glide over the words.

Kat, please let me explain. I didn't mean to betray you. I didn't. Please answer.

He used the word betray first, not me. Let the record show that. He knew what he did as soon as he did it. Let the record show that too.

I don't delete that message and move on to read more. They all say pretty much the same thing. I'm sorry. I didn't mean to be a douchecanoe. I want you to text back so I can have some reprieve from this horrible guilt.

Well, he didn't say those exact words, but the spirit of the messages is the same. He feels bad, and he wants me to make him feel better. Sorry, pal. Not going to happen.

Finally, I get to the last message he sent this morning. Probably right before he was about to walk into the studio for the first day of taping of Chef on Chef. Surprisingly, it's more of the same sadness and not a hint of gloating. Maybe he isn't a completely selfish tool.

Please read this and know I feel terrible, Kat. Did Sadie tell you I came to see you last night? I just want a chance to explain. I'm going to make this right. I promise.

Hmmmph. Don't make promises you can't keep, Alex.

I don't know why, but curiosity gets the better of me, and I begin typing a text to ask how he plans to make things right. Thankfully, just as I get the first word finished, I'm interrupted by my mother calling.

"Hey, Mom. What's up?" I say in my best fake chipper voice.

The last thing I want my mother to know is I'm feeling even the tiniest bit down. She'll blow everything completely out of proportion. It's her thing.

"I'm calling to see how things are going. They must keep banker's hours on TV. I thought this might go to voicemail since you'd be on the set. I just wanted to say good luck. No, no! That's bad. What do actors say? Oh, yes. Break a leg."

My mother is a genuinely kind soul, much like Sadie. I think it's why I gravitated toward my roommate the first time we met. The two of them wouldn't hurt a flea, and they truly mean well.

"About that, Mom," I say before taking a big bite of dry saltine. "I'm not going to be doing that reality show after all."

"Oh, honey. Why? I know you were so looking forward to that," she says, disappointment clinging to each word.

"Deidre called me back to work because a cook quit. It couldn't be avoided," I lie.

"I'm sorry. You must be so let down. That Deidre is one piece of work."

She's not wrong there. I'm sure I'll see just how bad she is in a few hours when I return to the kitchen.

"Please don't tell Daddy, okay?" I say as I jump off the barstool to get a drink from the refrigerator.

"Oh, I won't. He never liked the idea of you being on a reality show to begin with."

Great. So now he'll see me as a failure at something he didn't he approve of.

"Okay. Thanks, Mom."

As I chug a mouthful of water, my mother says, "I also called for a second reason. Your father and I will be coming to see you in two days.

He thought we should surprise you, but I put the kibosh to that. No young woman living on her own wants her parents to just drop in unexpectedly. Sometimes I swear that man was never young."

I nearly choke on the mixture of crackers and water at her news, sputtering pieces of food all over the refrigerator door. They're coming here? In two days? Whatever for?

Oh, more greatness. Now I get to enjoy my father's disapproval up close and in person. Super.

"That's great, Mom. What brings you to sunny Florida?" I ask, wishing I could ask how long they plan to stay.

I love my parents, and if it was only my mother coming, I wouldn't feel so utterly stressed out right now. But my father is another story. Every time we get together, I end up feeling like a complete and utter loser by the time he leaves.

"Oh! You know what we should do?" she says, avoiding the reason why they're coming to visit. "We should make reservations at that restaurant the three of us went to that one time. CK, was it?"

Can this get any worse?

"I'm not sure, Mom. I'm thinking Deidre is going to have me working every day until the end of time to make up for that week I wasn't in the kitchen."

"She can't schedule you for every hour of every day we're there, Katerina. I'll make the reservation today. I'll be sure to make it for a time you usually aren't at work. I wonder if they do lunch."

"To be honest, Mom, I think that restaurant closed," I say, lying through my teeth.

"What? CK? I can't believe that. They're the best restaurant in that area. No offense to yours, honey. Things just are what they are."

I can't help but chuckle at how kind she is about my feelings. I know where I work is not the best in town. I'm not even sure it's in the top fifty restaurants in the Tampa area.

"Sure, I know, but I heard something bad happened to their head chef."

Talk about wishful thinking.

"Oh, really? What happened?" she asks in a tone of genuine concern.

Smiling, I answer, "I heard he was mauled to death in a horrible alligator attack."

My mother gasps as I think to myself that a girl can dream. "Oh, that's terrible! I worry so much about you down there, honey. Those things can move very fast. I saw a show on the nature channel one night when I couldn't get to sleep, and I didn't have anything to help me. That creature was just sunning himself on a rock one minute and the next, bam! He got those fat little legs of his moving, and he scurried across a road to attack a man! Thank God he was able to get away fast enough because if he didn't, he would have been that alligator's lunch. I hope you're careful when you go out."

Every time my mother talks about things like that, I imagine her sitting in her beautiful home in Scarsdale right outside of New York City biting her nails down to the quick because she's convinced herself the entire state of Florida is literally crawling with swarms of alligators. I have never seen one in all the time I've lived here, but I doubt she'd believe that.

"It's okay, Mom. I always keep myself safe here. Sadie and I live on the fifth floor, and I don't think alligators climb up this high."

Breathing a sigh of relief, she says sweetly, "Good. I worry about you, Katerina."

"I'm fine, Mom. I can't wait to see you and Daddy. What time will you get here on Wednesday?"

Only two thirds of that is a lie. I can't wait to see her.

"We're taking an early flight out of JFK, so expect us before lunch. You know how your father is about airplane food, so we'll be looking for somewhere to eat as soon as we arrive."

"Okay, Mom. I'll be here, unless I'm at work. Just call me when you land. I love you."

"I love you too, Katerina. Is everything all right? You sounded strange just then when you said you loved me."

From out of nowhere, tears begin to prick at the

back of my eyes. "No, I'm fine," I lie. "Probably just pollen or something. Have a good flight."

"Thank you, honey. See you Wednesday! I know your father can't wait to see you again."

"Okay, Mom. See you then."

I set my phone down on the counter and let out a heavy sigh. I'm depressed from being thrown off the reality show and betrayed by a man I was actually starting to really care about. I have to go back to work and deal with Deidre, the boss from hell, who is likely going to relish making my life a nightmare after finding out I got expelled from the show.

And now my parents are coming for a visit, and no doubt, my mother is going to find out CK isn't closed. I'm going to have to sit through an entire dinner as my father raves about the food and talks about how wonderful it was when we met the head chef last time.

The same head chef who broke my heart and now thinks he can make things all better with a few texts.

Could my life get any worse?

CHAPTER SIX

 lex

"Welcome to the first day of taping," Shane announces from the center of the room. "Last week was to give you some time to get used to the set, but this week is the real deal."

Except for the pretend relationship thing.

Maria flashes us a big, toothy grin and says, "Now here's the most important thing we need you to know. Act naturally and be yourself, but remember that reality shows aren't about reality so much as what we want reality to be. So have a good time and don't forget your storylines."

The fact that she believes what she said makes this

all the more painful. Reality seems to be whatever they decide it needs to be for ratings. That's why we do so little cooking and so much romantic nonsense seems to be important.

"For this first day of the show, we're going to have you repeat last week's exercise with the person you're sharing your storyline with. Let's have a good time, and please, no poisoning this week," Shane says with a hearty laugh.

Everyone around me has a good time with that little slice of dark humor. Nice of him to joke about someone having to get their stomach pumped.

Already sick of all of this gung-ho attitude about nothing good, I clear my throat and ask, "How is Murphy, by the way? Is he out of the hospital?"

I suddenly feel all eyes on me, each person staring at me with surprise, as if they hadn't given another thought about the poor guy since the paramedics wheeled him out on that stretcher last week. Nice. No wonder not a single one of them seem bothered in the least by Maria's reality isn't reality except when we want it to be reality bullshit.

A million dollars sure can make people be shitty.

For a split second, I swear I see Maria's smile crack, but then it returns in full force as Shane says, "Oh, he's great! He's at home, and unfortunately, won't be able to return for this season of Chef on Chef, but he told me he wants to make sure everyone knows he wishes you good luck and he'll be watching with bated breath to find out who the winner is."

I nod, truly happy poor Murphy isn't permanently damaged from being poisoned by one of these people all clapping for his wonderful recovery at this moment. I intend on finding out who did it too since I know for sure neither Kat nor I was the one who put the poison in that dish.

How I'll unmask the criminal I have no idea. I'm no detective and have little interest in getting to know any of my fellow contestants any better than I do now, but I can keep my ears open and listen for any clue to the perpetrator.

It's the least I can do for Kat.

Contestants begin to pair off, and for a second, I wonder if I should go over to Emma's station just to be polite. Before I can decide anything, she rushes over full of enthusiasm and positions herself right next to me.

"Hey! This is so exciting, isn't it? You look great in your black chef's uniform. It's just like we're at work, except this is more fun."

"I prefer the white one I usually wear," I mumble.

"This time, you get to be the one taking orders," she says with far too much perkiness for me.

"Great."

"I promise I'll be easier to work with than Kat. I'm sure that was a challenge for you."

Her dig at the one contestant who had always been nice to her surprises me, and as she busies herself getting the area prepared for today's work, I wonder what the hell she has against Kat. I didn't hear everything they said to one another, but what I did catch seemed friendly and pleasant.

So what's with the backhanded way of talking about her now that she's gone? She can't honestly believe Kat poisoned that chicken bourguignon and sent Murphy to the emergency room.

"Kat was fine. I thought you two got along. She seemed very nice to you," I say as Emma lines up my knives, instantly irritating me. How does she not know touching another chef's knives isn't okay?

She looks up at me and smiles. "Oh, sure. Yeah, I guess. I just meant she didn't like you at all, so that must have made working together like you had to last week challenging, to say the least."

Something in the way her tone of voice sounds almost gleeful that Kat isn't here anymore grates on me. She had no problem with her, but somehow the way she was with me made her dislike the woman?

"She wasn't bad to work with at all. She's a talented chef. Because of that, I enjoyed cooking with her."

"Of course. I just know what she thought of you, so I wanted you to know you won't have to deal with any of that anger from me. I like you perfectly fine, Alex," she says, giving me a smile and doe eyes.

I've seen that look far too many times before not to understand what Emma's up to. I need to make it clear to her that this whole romantic storyline thing we have to do isn't real, no matter how Maria and Shane want to define reality.

"Good. I like you too, but none of what we're doing here is real life. Like you, I'm just on this show to win the million bucks. That's it."

While I speak, she nods like she understands, but the way she looks at me says she has something entirely different in mind for how things are going to work with us. I consider repeating myself, but what's the point? She's going to believe what she wants to believe no matter what I say.

Changing the subject, she says, "I think I want you to make something sweet for me, Alex."

My stomach instantly twists into a knot. Something sweet means dessert, my least favorite dishes to make. I'm not a pastry chef. Never have been. I leave that to people who like to work with delicate ingredients that tend to be incredibly fussy.

"Something sweet? Like what? I make a great pineapple ham with caramel sauce. Trust me. That's sweet enough to make dessert unnecessary."

Emma shakes her head and stares up at me in a way that screams she's flirting. "Nope. Guess again."

I don't want to guess. I'm already annoyed by how she was talking about Kat, and now I suspect she's going to have me create something with fucking phyllo dough. That shit never does what I want it to do. It's like working with tissue paper with how goddamned easily it tears. There's a very good reason I didn't become a pastry chef.

"Not really into guessing, so why don't you just tell me what you want me to make?"

From across the set, Maria yells, "Okay, everyone. You remember, Jonathan, right? Well, he's our host, so give him a big Chef on Chef welcome and get ready because we're about to start."

I'd wondered where he went to after not seeing him since that night he, Maria, and Shane showed up at CK to invite me onto this show. He didn't look like a game show host that night, but somehow today in his light grey suit and ultra tan that makes him look like he's spent the last month baking on the beach, he's the epitome of game show guy.

"Good to see everyone. I'm looking forward to working with all of you. Good luck!" he says with a big smile in that deep voice of his.

Maria waves her hands and announces, "Cameras rolling in three, two one! Enjoy!"

Instantly, I feel like I should paste a smile on my face, like it's elementary school and I just sat down on that hard wooden stool every photographer brought for school pictures. I don't, mainly because dread is filling me over what my new fake romantic interest has in store for today's challenge.

Emma, though, turns her smile up and begins

running her hand down my arm like we're at the club right before closing time and she's making her last play of the night. "Chocolate soufflé. Are you ready?"

Fuck me.

No, it doesn't involve phyllo dough, but it's just as bad. A fucking soufflé. And she thinks working with Kat was challenging. At least she wouldn't have wanted me to make some goddamned dessert that's likely to turn out like shit.

With a nod, I look down on the countertop next to the burners and see a recipe waiting for me. At least she doesn't expect me to do this by memory. The only time I've made a soufflé was back in culinary school, and that didn't turn out well. It was then that I knew desserts weren't my thing.

Cade's going to get a good laugh out of this when I tell him. Hailey does the sweet stuff. It's why I was so impressed by her baking. Desserts may look like the easiest part of the meal, but that's a mistake to believe that. They take a delicate hand, and I'm not known for that skill.

"I made sure to tell the crew to have the butter room temperature for you," Emma says as she points toward the dish of butter on the other side of the countertop.

"Thanks."

Eying up the block of semi-sweet chocolate sitting next to it, I wish she had them chop up enough for this damn soufflé. That she left for me. Great.

I reach over and grab it, setting it down on the cutting board in front of me. Christ, I hate working with sugary stuff. It gets all over you, and there's nothing like sticky gloves to make cooking a nightmare.

I keep the sweet stuff for sex only for good reason.

As I chop into the block of chocolate, Emma begins telling me about the last time she was on a show like this. "I did another reality show, and even though I didn't win, I got a lot of great ideas from it. That's where I came up with you making a soufflé, and since I love desserts, I figured why not make it chocolate?"

Even though I really prefer not to chatter away as I work, my curiosity gets the better of me and I ask, "Are you a pastry chef at the restaurant you work at?"

I glance over to see her shaking her head. "No, I'm an entremetier. I hope to be sous chef soon at my restaurant."

So she's in charge of soup, vegetable, and pasta dishes where she works. Odd that she wants me to make a dessert she likely couldn't make any better than I can. Then again, maybe that's the point. She does want to win the prize this time, I'm assuming, so making me look inept would go a long way toward that.

I get the feeling she'd love me to ask where she works as an entremetier chef, but I don't care enough to get into that conversation. All I want to do is make this soufflé and be done with it.

And her.

"So you're a head chef? That's impressive."

Nodding, I finish chopping the semi-sweet chocolate and make sure I have exactly the eight ounces the recipe calls for. Next up are three large egg yolks and four large egg whites. I grab what I need from the refrigerator and get to work separating the yolks and the whites. This is yet another reason I don't like making desserts. If it wasn't for the fact that the end product tasted so damn good, there'd be nothing good about making the final course of any meal.

"You're the head chef at CK, right?" Emma says as I busy myself with the egg work.

"Yep."

"I've never been there. I hear wonderful things about it, though. Do you like your owners? Mine are a dream to work for. In fact, they're the reason I went to culinary school."

As I finish the last egg yolk and white separation, I push the two glass bowls off to the side and move toward the sink to wash my hands. Emma's in my way, so for a moment we stand there pressed against one another before she finally steps back and lets me through.

"You didn't say if you like your owners or not, so I'm thinking you don't? That's a shame. It makes the job much easier if you get along with the people who own where you work."

I don't really want to make a point of telling her that the owners of my restaurant are my father and uncle, but she seems intent on continuing this conversation, so while I dry off my hands, I say, "You know how family is. Sometimes you like them. Sometimes you don't. But at the end of the day, you love them."

"Your family owns CK? Oh, my God! You are so lucky! I wish my parents owned a restaurant. I'd definitely be the head chef there."

I shoot her a nasty look, and she quickly adds, "Not that you got that job as head chef because of your family. I'm sure you're talented. Still, it's a nice perk, right?"

"Yeah."

An hour later, the chocolate soufflé she had me make looks pretty much like every dessert I've ever created. It falls before she can get Jonathan to come over and inspect it as he seems to have to do for every contestant cooking today, so when he examines it, there's clearly a look in his eyes that says he's not impressed in the least.

"Keeping a soufflé from collapsing can be challenging. As long as it tastes good, that's all that counts," he says like he wants to make sure my feelings aren't hurt.

Great. Now the game show host is pitying me.

"Okay, break!" Shane yells from the side of the set. "Be back in fifteen, everyone!"

I'm going to need at least fifteen minutes away from Emma and that goddamned soufflé to get in a better mood, but as I make a move toward the side door to escape for a little while, Maria calls me over to where she and Shane are standing looking distinctly unlike their usually happy and enthusiastic selves.

"What's up?" I ask as I stop a few feet away from them.

Far more serious than I've ever seen them before, the two producers sigh in tandem like they've rehearsed this moment. It's Shane who speaks first, and like his expression, he's not happy.

"Alex, we wanted to remind you of your romantic storyline with Emma. So far, we haven't seen much of anything concerning that today, and the cameras are rolling."

I open my mouth to complain about her insisting I make a fucking soufflé but stop myself. Emma isn't the issue. Either is the damn chocolate dessert that ending up falling and looking like shit.

The problem is I miss Kat and don't want to pretend to care for Emma or anyone else.

So I force a smile and promise to do better for them and the cameras. That's all it takes for them to be all happy once more.

By the time I get outside into the hot sun, all I can think of is texting Kat. For the umpteenth time, I tell her I'm sorry and want to talk to her to explain and send it off. Ten minutes later, my break is over, and she hasn't texted back.

If only there was a way I could convince her. I swear I'm not going to have a moment's happiness until I can.

CHAPTER SEVEN

at

Even though I swore I’d stay strong and not let Deidre get to me, I barely walk into the kitchen at Frederick’s before she starts in on me. I swear one day I’m going to walk out the door and never come back to this place.

But for now, I have to earn money and a bird in the hand is better than two in the bush. Or whatever the hell that saying is about having a job being better than having the possibility of a better job somewhere else. One pays real money I can use for my rent and to eat, and another only makes me feel better that someday this won’t be my life.

"So there's the reality TV star," Deidre calls across the kitchen at me. "How does it feel to be back in the real world, Kat?"

Lovely. Just fucking lovely, you evil Gorgon.

I give her a tiny smile I don't mean and head toward the breakroom to get dressed for my shift. When I get to my locker, I open it to find my white chef's jacket with my name embroidered on the breast is gone. Did I take it home when I knew I'd be gone for a week? No, that doesn't make any sense. The restaurant launders all our clothes we wear on our shifts, so I wouldn't bother taking it home.

Just as I turn to walk out into the kitchen and ask Deidre what's going on, she comes into the breakroom looking as pleased as punch about something. She's the type who rejoices when someone gets hurt, so maybe she saw a small child fall down out in the dining room.

"Before you ask, yes, your jacket is gone. You'll have to use one of the spares. Also, since you were gone enjoying life in Hollywood, I had to replace you, so now you're working on the line with salads."

Rage courses through me, and it takes every ounce of my energy to not flip out on her. "Salads? Why? I'm one of the chefs in this kitchen. Salads is where you put people who are just starting out."

"Well, I had to make sure the kitchen was properly staffed, and you chose to go off and do that reality show, so you really shouldn't be surprised, Kat. Also, your salary is now two dollars less since you aren't as responsible on salads as you had to be as an actual chef."

She decreased my pay by two dollars? What a bitch!

Anger bites at me, but I keep it at bay as I ask, "Why are you like this with me? You don't treat anyone else in this restaurant as bad as you treat me. Why? What have I ever done to you to deserve it?"

She rolls her beady eyes at me and straightens her toque over her frizzy blond hair, the name she insists we all call our chef's hats, as if calling it by a fancy name makes her more important. "Kat, I know because your last name is Truesdale that you think you have some special talent in this business, but you're just like everyone else. I treat you no differently than I do anyone else. The restaurant is going to be busy tonight, so get back into that kitchen and start making salads."

I knew that one time my father and mother came to eat here was a mistake. Ever since that night, Deidre has hated me even more than she used to. You'd swear I drop my father's name and his standing in our business into every damn conversation I have here. I don't think I've mentioned him a single time, so why she's so bothered by him and what is reputation is baffles me.

Spinning on her heel, she storms out of the breakroom as I feel tears begin to fill my eyes. No, I will not cry at work. If the man I actually care for doesn't get any more of my tears, this nasty bitch I can barely stand can't have any either.

Even more miserable than before I got here, I slip into my black and white checkered chef's pants and black work shoes and head toward the ladies' room to throw some cool water on my face. I can't work for the next eight hours in that kitchen if I don't calm down.

As I stare into the mirror above the sink, all I see is failure. I got kicked off Chef on Chef. I believed Alex and I had something when clearly we didn't have anything more than great sex. And now I'm relegated to making fucking salads in a kitchen where I used to make great food.

I fill my palms with cold water and splash my cheeks. It feels refreshing, but that's momentary. Not a minute after I walk back into the kitchen, I know I'll be hot under the collar and wanting to smack Deidre straight across the face.

That I can't because I'd lose my job is more frustrating than anything else.

"You can do this," I whisper to my reflection in front of me. "You have to do this. Deep breaths and stay calm."

Someone walks in as I'm giving myself a pep talk, so I quickly end the inspirational chat with my reflection. Turning to see who just joined me, I smile when I realize it's Heidi. One of the best servers Frederick's has, she's a beautiful blonde who never fails to brighten up a room.

"Hey, you!" she says, opening her arms to bring me in for a hug. "I missed you last week. I heard you aren't doing that show. Are you okay? I know it meant a lot to you."

I wave away the idea that being thrown off Chef on Chef bothers me. "It's okay. It wasn't really about cooking, to be honest, so I'm okay not being on it. I would have liked the million-dollar prize, though."

"Who wouldn't?" she says with a chuckle as she pulls me tightly to her.

I know it's silly since we're only work friends, but the feel of her arms around me makes me want to cry. I can't because I don't want everyone here to think Deidre got to me, but that's all I want to do as she holds me in her embrace.

When she releases me, she looks like she wants to cry too. "Hey, I wanted to tell you before anyone else does. Rafe is getting married."

She stops after dropping that bombshell, but I have the sense there's more. I know what the next sentence is, though, so she doesn't have to even say it.

But when she does, my chest feels like someone's run me clean through with a sword.

"To that girl who he…you know."

Yeah, I know. The girl he cheated on me with. The girl who was so desirable that he felt he needed to throw away a year-long relationship with me to be with her. That girl.

Every fiber of my being feels even worse than when Diedre told me I'd been demoted to salads and lost two dollars an hour of my salary, but I don't want Heidi to know that. So I smile and shrug like nothing about what Rafe and that girl do interests me.

"Well, let's hope they're happy," I manage to get out and sound almost sincere.

Heidi waits a moment to say anything, probably studying me to see if I'm actually okay with my ex-boyfriend marrying the one person in this world who hurts me the most. "Good, I'm glad you aren't feeling bad about that. He's a real shit, Kat. I always thought so, but when he screwed you over like that, I knew I was right about him all along. Let the two of them go off and be whatever they are together."

"Exactly! I need to get into the kitchen. Boss lady is on me hard already, and I'm barely back an hour."

Heidi, all too familiar with how rotten Deidre is since she's never been kind to a single server in all the time I've worked here, nods. "Don't let her get to you either."

"I'm going to grab a breath of fresh air and then it's back to the salt mine. I'll talk to you later, okay?"

I don't give her a chance to reply before I hurry out of the ladies' room toward the back door to get that air. My lungs feel like someone's stomping on them wearing work boots, and I don't know if I'll be able to keep standing if I don't take a few deep breaths.

Thankfully, no one is outside, so I'm alone. I tilt my head back and inhale deeply as I silently ask the question that's been on my mind for days. "God, I can't catch a break, can I? Just one?"

The blue sky above doesn't give me any answers, so I take another deep breath and turn to head into the building. Just then, my phone vibrates. It's probably another message from Alex. He sent me two already today.

I shouldn't read any more of them because they keep saying the same thing over and over, but right now, I can't help but feel happy to hear from him. I haven't forgiven him, but my white-hot anger has abated enough that I don't hate him anymore.

Sliding my phone out of my pants pocket, I open my messages and see it's not from Alex but Emma. That's okay too. She was the person I liked the most on the show, other than him, so maybe she wants to tell me she misses me. That would be thoughtful of her.

My eyes glide over the words as a feeling of utter dread fills me. Yes, she misses me, but she says she's making sure to keep an eye on Alex since they've been partnered together by Maria and Shane in a romantic storyline.

And to make things even worse, they're going out tomorrow on a date for the show.

Those words echo in my head as my brain puts them on repeat. A date for the show. Alex and Emma are going out on a date for the show.

So much for God cutting me a break.

CHAPTER EIGHT

lex

AFTER A DAY FILLED WITH BULLSHIT I'M NOT EVEN sure I want to deal with anymore for a chance at that million bucks, I sit on my balcony with a cold beer. I close my eyes as that first refreshing sip washes over my tongue and try to push away the day from my memory.

A few minutes of pure relaxation go by and I have to check my phone to see if Kat messaged me back. Nothing. She still hates me.

While I read over all the messages I've sent her, I'm interrupted by a phone call from a number I recognize as Maria's. Great. She and Shane probably want to chastise me for not being lovey-dovey enough with Emma after they talked to me the first time. Why I don't know. I smiled more. Hell, I even fed her some of the chocolate soufflé like she suggested because it would look convincing for the cameras. What do they want me to do? Throw her down on the countertop and do her right there in front of all of them?

I barely get a hello out when Maria breathlessly launches into what she wants to talk about. "Hi, Alex! This is so exciting! First of all, you don't have to come to the studio tomorrow. We have something even better planned for you. How does an off-sight event sound to you?"

Truthfully, it sounds terrible, but I pretend like her excitement is contagious and say, "Sounds great! What is it?"

"Well, Shane and I talked, and we thought you and Emma might be struggling a bit with your romantic storyline because of where you were today, so we're sending you out on a date! How cool is that?"

Not cool at all. Now I have to pretend to like this woman in a public setting? People are going to think we're really a couple, and God forbid Kat sees this if she watches the show.

"We'll send over a limo to pick you up and then you can pick her up before heading to the restaurant. We're so excited about this! I think it's going to be wonderful, so sleep in tomorrow morning and be ready for tomorrow night!"

"Sounds good. I'm assuming there will be cameras for this date, right?"

"Of course. It is a reality show, after all. So be ready. Have a great time! I can't wait to see the footage Randy shoots. It's going to be such a great part of the first episode, Alex. Night!"

She ends the call, and I take a gulp of beer, no longer satisfied with simply enjoying the taste. Now I want to get drunk off my ass so I can forget this is my life.

At least I don't have to wake up early tomorrow. That's about the only good side I can find to this entire thing. Maybe Cade and I can go out on the boat before he has to go into work.

Even though I know he's probably with Hailey, I'll call him tonight and convince him. It's been too long since we enjoyed some time out on the water.

Before I can do that, my phone vibrates, and I see it's my father calling. Maybe Cash and Savannah have eloped and sent the entire family into crisis. At least that would take my mind off my troubles for a little while as I talk him and my mother down off the ledge after finding out they won't get to experience their older child's big day.

"Alex, did you hear the good news?" he asks excitedly.

Perhaps I was right. Maybe my brother and his girlfriend did run off to get married.

"No. Did Cash and Savannah elope?"

"No! Jesus, don't let your mother hear you say that. She'll have to be given oxygen if she hears they did that."

"Okay. What's the good news?"

"You and your date are coming to CK tomorrow night, and there's going to be a film crew from Chef on Chef there doing scene shots tomorrow afternoon. I knew this reality show would be good for the restaurant. Did you suggest to them that the date occur at our restaurant?"

Oh, God. That's not great. Not only do I have to go out on a date with Emma, but now I have to take her to the place I work at and where I know everyone. Fucking special.

"No, Dad. I didn't suggest it, but I'm glad you're happy about it."

"I'm ecstatic, and even Kane is thrilled. We're going to make sure the place looks the best it's ever looked since there will be cameras there. Who's the date with?"

I let out a sigh, wishing I could say another name. "Her name is Emma. She's a contestant on the show. It's nothing really since it's only playacting like we actually like each other. The whole thing is pretend, Dad, but at least you and the restaurant might benefit from it."

"You don't sound like you're happy about this. Is something wrong? You're usually up for a good time,

Alex. What's going on? You've been unhappy for days."

For a moment, I consider telling him the truth about all that's happened between Kat and me, but I don't. It's too much to explain, and what's the point? She and I aren't any closer to getting back together.

"It's nothing, Dad. This reality show is just a lot of work. I wish I was back at CK, if you want to know the truth. The sooner that happens, the better. At least the restaurant gets something good out of it, though."

He hesitates for a few seconds and then quietly says, "If you want to talk about anything, you know you can always come to me, don't you?"

"Yeah, Dad. Thanks. I'm glad you're happy about tomorrow night. Tell Kane he needs to work on his smile. Everyone on this show seems very happy all the time."

That makes my father burst out into laughter. "Kane smile? That would ruin his entire reputation as the cranky owner. Maybe I can convince him to smirk a little. How's that sound?"

"Sounds good. I'll see you tomorrow night, Dad. I won't be able to get there early since they have a limo taking us to the restaurant, but if I can sneak back into the kitchen, I will."

They'll be lucky if I don't hide out in there for the entire date.

"A limo? Nice. Is it a black-tie date?"

That hadn't dawned on me when Maria told me

about it. Well, I have no intention of wearing a tux. If it was Kat, then yes, but for Emma? This pretend date will have to happen with me in my black suit.

"Not for me. I'll talk to you tomorrow, okay? Have a good night."

"Okay, son. Remember what I said about always being here to talk."

"Thanks, Dad. It'll be okay. Things always are for me."

And that right there is the problem. I'm not fine with okay anymore. I want more.

I want Kat.

The breeze coming off the water feels like it's heaven sent this morning, and I close my eyes for a few moments to enjoy the peace being out here gives me. Cade sits across from me relaxing after a hard night at work that included two brawls, one between a handful of women, and Stefan having a near meltdown on him about some behind-the-bar issue I didn't ask him to elaborate on.

We both needed to get away, so he jumped at the chance to hang out with me on the boat for a few hours this morning, even though it meant cutting into his sleep. I especially need this so I can get figure out what to do about the situation with Kat.

"So, are you planning on telling me what the hell is

going on with you, or do I get to be like the rest of the family and just guess? Personally, I thought we were closer than that," Cade says with more than a hint of sarcasm.

I open my eyes and blow the air out of my lungs as I look up at the crystal blue cloudless sky. I haven't told a soul what's wrong, other than the little I told my grandmother, but it feels like I've thought about it every second of every day since I watched Kat drive out of the studio parking lot in tears.

"We are. You're my best friend. You know, I could say the same thing about you since you and I barely see each other anymore. I thought we were closer than that."

He smiles and gives me a nod like he understands what I'm not saying. It's not that I'm jealous. I'm glad Cade found someone, and Hailey's the best. I couldn't have picked a better woman for him. It's just that after our entire lives being like inseparable twins, the past year has been a hard change to get used to.

"Point taken. I have been spending a lot of time with Hailey and ignoring hanging out with you. I guess it's that I thought I needed to be with her since we're a couple now and my friendship with you could handle a little time on the back burner. I wasn't trying to be a dick, Alex."

I shrug and wave away that idea. "You weren't being a dick. Well, no more than you usually are since it's your nature to be a dick," I say with a chuckle.

"Fuck you, Eye Candy. As if you're any different," he responds, smiling.

Cade and I have always joked around with each other like this, but there's a little truth in everything we say to each other. He was being a dick, and I've had my moments of dickiness, to be sure.

We sit in silence for a few moments before I say, "I think I've been feeling like the odd man out lately. I mean, with you, Cash, and Liam all settled down, I got lost in my work. So if I'm being honest, I'm probably as much to blame for us not hanging out as you are, although you are always with your girlfriend."

A warm breeze flows over me, and I remember how much I love being out here on the boat. It has been too long since we hung out like this, and whether it's his being with Hailey or my diving into work, I need this time out here with my best friend.

"So you still haven't told me what's changed with you, Alex. You're always a good time, but at Grandma's, you practically bit everyone's head off every time we asked you what was going on. Is it something involving work, and that's why you haven't said what's wrong?"

Shaking my head, I think about how I wish it was something at the restaurant. That I could handle. No, this is definitely not easy like that.

"Is it the reality show? I really thought you'd be killer on that, man. You've got the looks, the charm, and everything else reality shows seem to look for.

They asked you to be on the show, for God's sake, so they must have thought the same thing. Is it bad?"

The mere mention of that makes my entire body tense up. God, I hate that show now. If it wasn't for the chance that I could win the prize money, I'd bail today and deal with my father's disappointment. Then again, after my less than stellar showing with that damn soufflé, maybe I shouldn't think I have much of a chance anymore.

I stand up to grab a bottle of water out of the cooler and toss one to Cade. "It sucks. No kidding, man. It sucks so fucking bad. Everything is so fake. I hate that kind of shit. I should have followed my gut and said no."

A sheepish expression settles into Cade's face. "Except I convinced you to do it. I had no idea it would be so bad. I figured you'd be great at it, but I do have to say I don't really watch those kinds of shows."

The cold water rolls down my throat, cooling me off from the hour or so we've been in the sun. "I don't do fake, and that's all this show is. There is no reality with these people. That's not how I work. I admit I've done some things in my life I'm not too proud of, but none of it has ever been fake. If I'm talking to someone, I'm real. If I'm with a woman, she's getting the real me. I don't like pretending. That takes the fun out of things."

Cade nods as I complain about what I truly hate about the show, and when I finish, he says, "You know, I don't think I've ever thought about things that way, but you aren't fake. You like having a good time, and for you, that means being real. Being around all that fakeness all day must be exhausting."

"It is. I hate it. Nobody's real and nothing we're doing is real."

I hesitate for a moment before adding, "But there was this one person I spent time with who wasn't like that. She's as real as it gets, and I liked being with her."

"This story doesn't sound like it ends well. What happened?"

So tired of keeping it to myself, I finally admit what I did to someone else. "It all went to shit because of something I did. I fucked up, and the worst part is, I really liked her."

With a smile, Cade says, "I find it hard to believe you fucked up that bad. If she's that real and you're who you always are, it sounds like you should have been good together."

"I did. I really fucked up," I say, hanging my head. I've spent days beating myself up over this, and to finally have the chance to tell Cade what I did actually feels like a relief.

"So fix it. Use that old Alex charm to convince her that what you did wasn't that bad."

Shaking my head, I have to smile. Cade knows me better than anyone else in the world, and it's nice to know he believes that much in me. The problem is charm isn't going to fix this problem.

"It was Kat. She's a chef like me. I thought it could go somewhere. I really did."

Cade's face registers his shock. "Are we talking something serious? You haven't been anywhere close to that since Hailey's friend Meadow."

I nod, happy to finally admit the truth. "Yeah, I thought it could be serious."

"Well, why can't it now?"

I slam the water bottle off the railing on the side of the boat and snap, "Because I fucked up! Weren't you listening to a word I said? I fucked up royally, as in she never wants to see me again."

"Did you cheat on her? I know you don't think of it as cheating since you're never exclusive, but I've learned a lot since I've been with Hailey, and oddly enough, women always have a problem with other women being in the picture. It wasn't the threesome, was it? That would make someone mad."

"No, it wasn't cheating," I admit as I sit down across from him again.

"Then what the hell did you do?" Cade asks in frustration, clearly tired of my beating around the bush.

It's just that actually admitting I was such a shit, even to my best friend who knows all the bad parts of me, isn't easy. I'm not exactly proud of what I did.

"I had a choice to make, and I made the wrong one."

Cade levels a look of pure impatience on me and grimaces. "Women always accept your apologies, man. I think you might be overthinking this a bit. But I can't help here if you don't give me specifics. Trust me. I've seen you do some pretty wild shit, Alex. I doubt you could shock me. So hit me with it. What did you do that was so terrible that this woman never wants to see you again?"

Swallowing hard, I try to come up with a way to tell him about how bad I fucked up but there's no prettying this up. I was an asshole. No ifs, ands, or buts about it.

"A dish she made with me turned out to make another contestant sick. The producers accused her of intentionally trying to poison him, but that's impossible since she and I were together at my place when it supposedly happened. If I had told them that, they may have kept her on the show, although to be honest I'm not even sure of that anymore since I eventually told them the truth and they didn't care. But I didn't say a word because I didn't want to lose my chance at the million dollars. She got kicked off the show, and now she can't forgive me for not speaking up and defending her."

He doesn't say a word for a long time, simply shaking his head as he silently condemns me. I deserve it. I should have said something when they accused her, something that would have proven she couldn't have come back to the studio that night and poisoned anything.

Finally, he shrugs and says, "Sounds like you wanted the money more than you wanted her."

"Thanks. That helps a lot."

"I'm just stating the obvious. So go find another one. You've never had a problem with that. Find another one to forget this one."

Jesus, is he not fucking listening?

"What if I said that about Hailey when you fucked up with her?" I snap, jumping up out of my seat to walk away before we get into a damn fistfight over this.

My outburst surprises him into silence for a few minutes, but after a while, he walks over to where I'm standing looking out at the water. "What are you saying? Are you saying you care about her? Are you in love with her?"

Every word comes out of his mouth on a wave of disbelief, like even my best friend can't believe I could actually care for a woman like that. Am I truly only a hedonistic manwhore? Doesn't Cade, of all people, believe I'm capable of truly caring for a woman?

But then again, I guess it's not that surprising. I've never talked about anyone like this before.

I look over at him and see him waiting for my answer. "I don't know. I've never loved anyone before."

He glances up and down like he's inspecting me for some evidence of caring and shakes his head. "Sad, lost, and it looks like you haven't slept well in days. Looks like love to me."

"I thought love made people happy, made them glow."

Cade laughs in my face. "Only in the movies. Real life love doesn't look anything like that. So what are you going to do?"

"She won't even answer my texts. I tried calling too, and I even went over to her apartment. She won't talk to me."

"You sure you love this woman? She seems immune to your charms. I never pictured the person you'd end up with would be able to deny the one thing that never fails for you."

I roll my eyes in disgust. "Christ, Cade, you're not helpful at all. I'm trying to figure out what to do, and you're talking about the one thing she hates about me. Actually, she hates everything about me now, but I don't think she's ever been crazy about my charm."

"Fine. Here's the reality. You can either forget her and move on or do whatever it takes to win her back. Those are your choices. Sorry if that's not helpful."

I stare out at the water and sigh. He's right. There is no third choice. I just don't know what to do to get her to see I deserve another chance.

CHAPTER NINE

lex

I CHECK MY PHONE TO SEE IF KAT TEXTED BACK after my last message but see nothing. Maybe she hasn't seen it yet. That could be possible, right?

After talking to Cade this morning, I took his advice to heart. Either I forget her, or I fight for her. There's nothing else I can do.

So, I sent her a text to tell her I'll be coming over to see her tonight. She can choose not to answer the door, but I'm perfectly fine saying what I have to say to her through the door for all her neighbors to hear. It's her choice.

I'm not sure that's what I should have done, but I've never had to fight for someone before. Either it works, or it blows up in my face and I have to go with plan B. As to what that plan is, I have no idea.

Maybe stand outside her apartment building and blare music like that guy does in that movie my mother loves? I don't think anyone does that anymore, especially since I can't imagine holding a goddamned stereo above my head like that. Where would someone even find something like that?

As all of these thoughts run through my head, the limo rushes down the street toward Emma's place and I sit in the backseat wishing I was anywhere else but here right now. The producers made sure to cover everything, including leaving us a bottle of chilled champagne, so I pop the cork and pour myself a glass, needing something to take the edge off how much I don't want to do this date tonight.

The cameraman slides open the partition between the front seat and where I sit and pokes his head through. "We're here."

I don't say anything since I'm not sure why he needed to tell me that little fact. He stares at me like I'm forgetting something important and finally points at the door.

"You need to go up to her door. Also, I think you were supposed to wait for her to break open the champagne."

Fucking terrific. They're making me do the whole thoughtful suitor act.

Downing the last of my champagne, I set the empty flute in the ice and give him a smile. "Oh, well."

"I'll be back there with you two from this point on. Just in case you didn't realize that."

While I fling the limo door open, I mumble, "I didn't, but whatever. Not exactly the kind of threesome I generally enjoy, though."

Behind me, I hear Randy chuckle before I slam the car door shut. I don't think I've ever been so disinterested in a date in my entire life. Not even that one time my parents made me go out with that weird girl with braces who only talked about Lord of the Rings because her mother had met my mother at yoga class and the two of them were sure it would be good for their seventh-grade children to go to the school dance together. Even then I didn't care as little as I do right now.

I hear footsteps and turn around to see Randy with his camera ready for Emma to open the door. Seriously?

"I didn't know you would be filming every minute of this date. I thought it would be mostly at the restaurant," I say at the bottom of the steps leading to her front door.

He pushes his glasses up the bridge of his nose and laughs. "Maria and Shane want every moment of tonight. From the first second you see each other to when you say goodnight."

"Fantastic."

Randy picks up on my sarcasm and laughs again. Like his bosses, he always seems too fucking happy. "They particularly love when I get embarrassing moments, so fair warning."

Fucking lovely.

"Well, here goes. Make sure you get this because I'm not repeating it a second time," I say as I begin to walk up to Emma's front door.

Unlike Kat, she lives in a white stucco house that looks like it cost a fortune. She can't afford this on a chef's salary, especially considering the type of chef she is, so I'm assuming it's a friend's or her family's home?

God, I hope there isn't a group of people standing behind this door with her. It'll be that seventh-grade date all over again.

I give a quick knock and silently wish someone would answer and say Emma decided to bail on the whole date thing tonight. That way I could head straight to Kat's apartment and begin to convince her she should give me another chance.

My wish goes unfulfilled, and Emma appears in front of me dressed in a black dress that barely comes to the middle of her thighs and is cut so low that I'm getting a healthy view of her breasts. I'm surprised since I've never seen her dressed in anything but yoga pants and t-shirts and then our chef's uniforms yesterday when taping of Chef on Chef began. She's quite beautiful now that I see her like this, and if I wasn't so preoccupied with another woman, I might consider sleeping with her.

She twirls around to show me a three-hundred-and-sixty-degree view of her and her tiny black dress that hides next to nothing. "What do you think? Do you think it'll look good on camera?" she asks, genuinely concerned about that.

"It looks great. You look very nice, Emma. Ready?"

She turns back to say something to another person in the house, and I steel myself for the possibility that she's going to introduce me to someone. Oh, God. I do not want to have to meet parents tonight.

Thankfully, she doesn't invite me in or them to the door, and a few seconds later, she practically bounces down the stairs. Holding her hand out when she reaches the sidewalk, she smiles and says, "Come on! We have a date to get to, Alex."

I glance over at Randy smiling as he films this entire scene and wonder how downright surly I must look right now. Forcing a smile, I walk down to her and take her hand in mine.

"Let's go have a good time."

Too bad that didn't sound terribly convincing.

Emma squeezes my hand and smiles up at me. "I can't wait to visit your restaurant, Alex. This will be my first time going there."

For a second or two, I wonder why she's telling me that since she already mentioned she'd never been to

CK before the other day. Then I remember what she's clearly far more focused on than me tonight—we're on camera.

"I think you're going to love it," I say, actually sounding interested in this date for the first time. What I'm actually interested in is my restaurant. That I care about. This whole reality show fake date thing I don't give a damn about.

As we walk to the limo, she asks, "Do you have a favorite dish you'd suggest I try?"

"We make a great steak, but if you want something in the seafood area, I'd say the salmon or the sea bass."

When I open the limo door for her to get in, she asks, "Do you have anything vegetarian?"

I nod, even as the thought of making my least favorite entrée flashes in my mind. "The mushroom risotto with truffle oil is one of the favorites."

"Mmmm…that sounds delicious. I can't wait to get there!"

She climbs in as Randy gets close for a shot of her taking a seat in the back of the limo and then turns toward me. "You get in and I'll shoot the two of you having a glass of champagne together."

Sighing, I get in and wonder how anyone could possibly think anything about this is real. They're going to have to do some hardcore editing to make this seem even close to believable.

Emma has a glass of champagne poured for me

when I sit down, so I take it and thank her before raising my glass in a toast. "To a wonderful evening."

She does the whole clinking our glasses thing, and then when Randy has gotten enough shots of us drinking, the limo driver thankfully begins driving toward the restaurant. It's all so scripted and awkward, but Emma seems perfectly happy to chat away about food and the weather and anything else that pops into her head.

By the time we reach CK, I'm exhausted, and I haven't even started to pretend I'm having a good time yet. I can only imagine how dead tired I'll be after this night is over.

I escort her into the building, seeing the maître d' Alphonso as soon as we walk to desk. He's clearly been warned this is happening because I don't think I've ever seen him this animated before, waving us over and then nearly bowing when I introduce Emma to him.

"What a pleasure it is to have you visit us, miss. Your table is ready, so if the two of you will follow me."

We do just that, along with Randy and his camera, and I see my father and Kane standing off to the side of a table in the center of the room. Fuck. Having to be here on a pretend date is bad enough, but making us center stage has to be my father's idea.

It's like he doesn't know me at all.

"Welcome to CK. It's wonderful to have you here

to dine with us tonight," my father says with a smile that goes ear to ear. Even Kane looks happy.

Emma swivels her head to look around the room and then back at him. "Oh, thank you. Your restaurant is beautiful. You must be so proud."

Knowing Randy is busy filming everyone but me at the moment, I give my father and Kane my best glare to let them know they need to disappear. Thankfully, they understand the look I give them and politely excuse themselves.

Once we're seated with menus, I lean over the table and whisper to Emma, "Excuse me for a minute. I just want to check on that mushroom risotto."

"Oh, okay. Thank you. That's very thoughtful of you, Alex."

As I move away from the table, Randy begins to follow me, but I quickly put an end to that. Raising my hand, I stop him. "Stay with her. I'll be right back."

"But..."

He doesn't get another word out before I shake my head. "No. Trust me. Stay with her."

This time he listens and moves back to the table to film her as she decides what to try for an appetizer while I hurry over to where my father and Kane stand near the door to the kitchen. They look as proud as peacocks, but all I can think is why did they make sure every person in the restaurant can see what we're doing here tonight?

"You look great, Alex," my father says as he

straightens my tie. "And your date is lovely. What's her name?"

"Emma and she's not my date. What the hell are you doing seating us in the damn center of the entire dining room? It's not bad enough this whole farce is happening, but now you have to make us the focal point of everyone here?" I ask him and my uncle.

"What's the problem? I thought this would be a good idea," my father says with a sly smile that tells me he knows exactly what the damn problem is.

"For what it's worth, I told him to put you two at the best table near the windows. It's more romantic," Kane says, like he's helping the situation.

"This isn't a fucking date! It's a reality TV show pretend date between two people competing against one another who have to playact like they're interested in one another for the goddamned camera. Not a damn date!"

Both men stare at me in shock. You'd swear these people have never met me before. I've never once brought a woman to CK on a date. Do they actually think I'm going to start tonight?

"Do you want me to change your seat?" my father asks half-heartedly.

I glance over at Emma and see Randy moving around the table like he's trying to get all angles of her. Looking back at my father, I shake my head. "No, but be prepared. Your other guests are going to have shitty experiences here tonight because he's going to be doing that nonsense right there the whole time."

That makes my father rethink his decision to put us at that center table. Before I can stop him, he walks over to Emma and gestures toward the table Kane had suggested in the first place.

Nudging me, my uncle gives me a wink. "See? He'll fix it and everything will be okay. I don't think I've ever seen you this unhappy, Alex. First at Alexandria's and now here tonight. Is everything all right?"

I quickly tick off all the reasons everything is absolutely not all right, but I decide not to say anything to him. "I hate living my life in a fishbowl, and that's what tonight feels like. I just need this to get done with so I can go back to my life."

"She's very beautiful," he says, almost as a consolation. "At least there's that."

He's right. It could be worse. She could look like a troll and snort liquid out of her nose when she laughs. That would definitely be worse.

"Yeah. I guess. Kane, do me a favor, would you? Keep my father busy while this whole thing is going on, okay?"

His blue eyes light up like I said something funny. "It's his first time seeing you on a date, Alex. Give the guy a break."

Then it dawns on me. Kane's right. Other than that seventh-grade nightmare of a date with that weird girl, this is the first time he's even met a woman I'm supposedly dating. Still, I can't have him hovering over us all night. That will only encourage Emma to think this is an actual date.

"Just keep him away, please?"

With a smile that tells me he thinks this pretend date is real, Kane nods. "Okay. I'll keep him occupied."

"Thanks. I guess I need to get this meal started so it can end."

"That's the way to think about it," he says with a laugh.

Family. I usually love mine, but that's because they're never in my actual life outside of this restaurant and family get-togethers. Right now, all I'm feeling is this is going to be as bad a disaster as that date with Lord of the Rings girl.

An hour later and our dinner is finished, thankfully. Emma hasn't been terrible, and there were moments that I didn't dislike being here with her. It's not her fault. She's just not the woman I want to be with tonight or any other night, for that matter.

"Are we going to have dessert?" she asks as the server hands us cards with tonight's dessert offerings.

"Sure. We don't have any soufflés, but the German chocolate cake is pretty great. I've only had it once, but I can recommend it," I say with a rare smile.

Her expression falls at my mention of the soufflé. "You're angry with me because I had you make that chocolate soufflé, aren't you? I just wanted to give you something you don't usually make. Please don't be mad at me."

I try to avoid looking at her big eyes full of worry that I'm upset with her, but it's impossible. Feeling like shit, I shake my head and smile.

"It's okay. I just wish it didn't fall."

The concern disappears from her face, replaced by real happiness when she hears I'm not angry with her. "I tried it, and it tasted great. I made sure to tell Jonathan that too, so don't worry. It didn't go against you."

"Thanks."

Out of the corner of my eye, I see someone who looks familiar. Turning to see who it is, I half expect it to be another member of the March family like my mother or Cade, but to my surprise, I see Kat seated at the bar. Dressed in a long black dress, she looks beautiful.

Damnit! This can't be good for any chance of getting her back. The look on her face is nothing short of sad. Fuck, why the hell is she here?

I need to talk to her. I can't let her think this is a real date. I wanted a chance to explain myself, and here it is, so I need to catch her before she leaves.

Leaning over, I say to Emma, "I need to speak to my father about something. Do me a favor and order me the chocolate cake when you order dessert, okay?"

She nods enthusiastically, and I walk over toward

the service area next to the kitchen to make it seem like I'm actually going to speak to my father, all the while keeping my eye on Kat. When she sees me moving toward her, she hurriedly gets up to leave, just as I suspected she would.

This may be my only chance. I can't let her leave without hearing me out.

So I hurry behind her and catch her just as she makes her way out into the lobby. "Kat, wait!"

She doesn't respond, so I grab her arm to stop her. When she spins around, I see nothing but pure hurt in her beautiful eyes. "Don't let me interrupt your date, Alex."

"It's not a date. Well, it is, but not a real one."

Fuck, I'm getting lost in the useless details. I need to focus on what I want to tell her. "Forget that. Come with me. Please? I want to talk to you but not here."

When she doesn't answer, I take that as a yes and pull her back into the restaurant just in time to see Randy on his way over to me filming the entire thing. Jesus, is this guy for real?

I need to figure out where the hell we can find some privacy in this restaurant. My father's office will have to do, so I tug her into the hallway next to the kitchen and hurry her away from Randy and his damn camera.

"Where are you taking me? Let me go!"

"Just give me a few minutes. That's all I ask, okay?"

She doesn't try to leave, so that's something. Thankfully, Randy doesn't follow us, and when I slam the office door behind us, I finally have her all to myself to say everything that's been on my mind for the past few days. Now I just have to hope she'll be willing to listen and not bolt before I finish.

"You look beautiful, Kat. I'm so happy to see you here tonight."

Glaring up at me, she practically growls when she says, "Whatever you're planning on saying, Alex, it doesn't matter. All that matters is what you did and that you're having the night of your life with Emma."

Not a good start, but maybe that means things can only get better.

CHAPTER TEN

at

I DON'T WANT TO FOCUS ON HOW GORGEOUS HE looks standing here in this black suit that seems to fit every inch of his body perfectly, but I can't help myself. If it had been months since I was next to him naked in bed or even weeks, maybe my mind wouldn't go to that place, but it's too soon and he's right here, so close and looking so good.

No! I can't let him and that beautiful body of his make me forget what he did and what I just witnessed for the past half hour.

"Let me out of here, Alex. I want to leave."

As I try to push past him, he stops me by holding

my arm. "Kat, please let me explain. This isn't what it looks like. I swear."

God, he must think I'm some kind of idiot. I know what's going on out there at the table. I have eyes.

Even though I know it's a mistake, I look up at him and practically get lost in those luscious brown eyes of his. "Aren't you on a date with Emma? I hear you two are an item now on the show. Good for you. She's a nice person. Too bad for her, though."

That's my hurt talking, but since the only other choice is to let my feelings for him come out, better to stay with the hurt.

"Kat, I'm sorry. I've been texting and calling and even coming over to your apartment to tell you that. Did you get any of my texts? Did Sadie tell you I stopped by?"

His voice sounds almost frantic, like he's worried I won't listen to him give the same excuses he's given for days. Or maybe he's more worried that he wasted all his precious time typing out those messages pleading with me to believe how sorry he is.

Sorry enough to go out on a date with another woman just days after we slept together. God, I really am an idiot. First, I was a shrew, and now I've graduated to idiot. Or maybe that's a demotion. This certainly would be the week for that.

"I read them all. So what? You're sorry that at the moment I needed you the most in that studio, when everyone was looking at me like I was some kind of criminal, you didn't do what someone good would do. Great. Thanks. With that and two bucks, I can grab a soda on my way home tonight."

His eyes soften, and I don't know if it's possible, but I swear he grows even more gorgeous right in front of me. "I know I fucked up. I want to fix it. I tried to yesterday. I went to Maria and Shane and told them everything—about how you were at my place that night and how you couldn't have been at the studio to put anything in that food. I confessed everything."

My spirits soar for a moment, but then they crash down to earth again. Maria and Shane haven't called me to come back to the show, and if he had actually said a word to them about my being innocent because we were together, they would have.

"I don't believe you. They haven't contacted me, and don't you think they would if they knew the truth?"

And then I see a sheepish look come over him and know what happened.

"Oh, I get it. You told them, but since you're the golden boy, they didn't care. In fact, they wanted to reward you for your honesty by giving you a romantic storyline with Emma. How very nice for you, Alex March. Tell me, how was I wrong about you in the first place?"

I feel tears beginning to sting the back of my eyes, but I will not cry here in this office in the finest restaurant in town where this man works and is probably loved by everyone here. I won't let him see how much all that's happened between us hurts me.

"Listen to me, please. I don't know why they didn't throw me off the show. I was prepared for them to do that. I would have gladly left since now that you aren't there it isn't anything but bullshit fake nonsense. But I did tell them the entire truth. I know you didn't poison anyone."

Pushing hard against his chest, I try to get him away from me, but he doesn't budge. So I step back because him standing so near to me is fucking with my ability to stay angry.

He comes with me, though, staring down into my eyes with so much kindness in his that I want to believe him. I can't, though. I saw what happens when you fall for Alex March.

"How do you know I didn't do it? We barely know each other. It's not like we have a long history together. We've known each other for just over a week, for God's sake. I guess a day or two longer if you count our meeting at Club X, but we aren't close. I mean, clearly you aren't that lost without me since you're out there having a grand old time with Emma, right?"

Alex takes my hands in his and holds them tightly, like he's afraid if he doesn't keep me right there I'll disappear from his life completely. "I can't tell you how I know. I just do, Kat. And no, we haven't known each other for long, but there's something about you that makes me feel like we've known one another for a lifetime. That's why I kept texting and came over to your apartment. I feel like something important has been taken away from my world, and I want it back."

I look down at my hands and try to decipher what he means by all of that. "So what are you saying? You know things because of what? Some secret ability that makes you think you understand me? Because you don't. Someone like you could never really get someone like me."

"That's not true. You and I are alike in a lot of ways, and for the first time in my life, I felt like I could be truly myself. I never realized all those other times I was with women that there could be anything more than just the physical, but with you, I found that extra thing. It's not some secret ability. It's the way you made me feel when you smiled at me or laughed at something I said. No other woman has ever made me want the things you did."

I so wish what he's saying could be true, but I'm the kind of person the Alex Marches of the world walk over on their way to the top. The kind of woman who gets pushed aside for others or a million dollars.

Yanking my hands from his hold, I turn away as the tears become too much to hold back. "Do you know when I had to return to work that I was demoted because I was thrown off that show? You're now looking at the salad prep at Frederick's instead of one of the chefs. And yes, that comes with a decrease in my salary, just in case you're wondering. That's the cherry on top of the past week I've had. When have you ever had to deal with anything like that, Mr. We're So Alike?"

He's silent for a long moment as I will the tears to go away so I don't look like some pathetic thing standing here in front of him. He has no clue how much I wish we were alike. Maybe then I wouldn't be sitting at the bar watching him on a date while I try to figure out a way to feel good about my life again.

"I'm sorry. That's not right. I'd never do that to any of my chefs here. I wish you didn't have to deal with that."

It's stupid, but somehow him saying he would never do that to the people he works with makes any control I have evaporate. The tears come, even as I wish they wouldn't, and I cover my face with my hands, ashamed of how sad I must look.

"Please don't say anything else. It's bad enough that's my reality. I don't want your pity too," I say through the sobs.

He pulls me to him and wraps his strong arms around me, and for a tiny moment in time, I am the happiest version of myself that's ever existed. I feel safe and cared for like never before.

Above me, he remains quiet while I cry against his chest until he whispers, "It's not pity. I swear. It's what someone who cares says when they hear you've had a bad day."

Tilting my head back, I see him looking down at me and don't notice any pity in his expression. Maybe he's telling the truth.

But that doesn't change what he did.

"Why didn't you speak up and tell Maria and Shane the truth when everything happened?"

His face twists into a scowl, and I don't know if it's for me or the memory of what he did. Turning his head, he avoids my gaze when he answers, "I don't know. I should have. I knew it as soon as I saw your face."

"I lost everything because of what you didn't do. How can I ever forget that?"

Alex lets his hands fall from around me and steps back just as the office door flies open. The man I assume is one of the owners barges in looking flustered and angry.

"Alex, what the hell is going on? Why are you in here when that beautiful woman is sitting out at that table all by herself and that cameraman is walking around my restaurant like he's looking for something?"

"Dad, not now."

The man with the dark hair and crystal blue eyes who doesn't look like Alex turns to face me. For a second, he doesn't react, but then a slow smile lights up his expression.

"I'm sorry. I didn't realize Alex wasn't in here alone." Extending his hand, he says, "I'm Cassian March, Alex's father and one of the owners here."

I shake his hand and try to keep my emotions in check as I say, "Hi. I'm Kat Truesdale. I'm…"

Unsure how to finish that statement since I'm not sure what I am to Alex, I hesitate and then finally say, "I'm just leaving. It was nice to meet you, Cassian."

Before Alex can catch me, I rush out, embarrassed and sad because what I told Alex was true. I don't know how I can forget what he did or forgive him.

CHAPTER ELEVEN

lex

I HURRY OUT AFTER KAT TO STOP HER, BUT SHE'S gone by the time I reach the dining room. I run to the front door to see if I can catch her in the parking lot, but it's no use. She's nowhere to be found.

Disgusted that my one opportunity to convince her to give me another chance has come to nothing, I march back to my father's office with Randy following close behind. I swear if this guy doesn't find someone else to film, I'm going to crush that damn camera of his with my bare hands.

"Dude, read the fucking room. I'll be out in a few minutes. You can get all the footage you want then," I snap just before slamming my father's office door in his face.

All I want is a few moments of silence. However, since my father's sitting at his desk waiting for me, that's not going to happen.

"Alex, who was that woman in here with you? And why was she crying?"

I collapse into the chair in front of his desk and pinch the bridge of my nose to stop the headache that's starting to form behind my eyes. "Her name is Kat. She was a contestant on that goddamned reality show just like my date is."

"What do you mean was? What happened? I thought the show just started taping yesterday," he says in his usual curious way.

My father isn't going to let this be. Fucking terrific. I could just leave, but that would mean I'd have to go rejoin Emma on this ridiculous date of ours. I know I'll have to go out there eventually, but at this very moment, I'm not in a place where I want every emotion I'm experiencing to be filmed for the entire world to see.

I take a deep breath and let it out of my lungs in a hard exhale. "She got kicked off the show because of me. More like because of something I didn't do, not something I did."

"Is that why she was here tonight? I get the feeling she's pretty angry with you."

"You think?" I snap.

Fuck, I need to get my shit together. Now I'm being a dick to my father, and he didn't do anything wrong.

I see the confusion in his eyes as he waits for me to say something else. I guess without all the details, this night looks like a complete clusterfuck.

"Sorry. This has been a nightmare, this whole reality show."

"Is this what's been bothering you?"

I hang my head, wishing it was just one thing. "Kat got thrown off the show because something she cooked made another contestant sick. He had to be taken to the hospital to get his stomach pumped, and the doctors said he was poisoned. But she couldn't have done that because when they claim she was at the studio putting it in the dish she was with me at my place. I didn't say anything when they first accused her because it's in our contracts that we aren't allowed to fraternize with other contestants."

When I finally finish, I take a deep breath and let it out in a rush. "I fucked up, Dad."

"This looks like a lot more than just you feeling bad about someone getting poisoned or you not speaking up when you should have. Are you and this woman more than just casual friends?"

The way he says that like it's code for fuck buddies or people I randomly sleep with makes me smile, and I look up to see him smiling too. "I think we could have been more than just the once we were together, but she can't forgive me for letting her down. I guess I can see her point, but every time I try to show her I'm not that selfish prick she thinks I am, something messes it up. Either she doesn't answer my texts and calls or she won't come to the door when I go to her apartment."

"Or I walk in on you as you're talking."

"It's okay," I say with a shrug, at least hoping I can make him feel better tonight. That'll be one person. Two if you count Emma, but I'm sure I'm making her unhappy right now since I'm not out there with her.

"You know, I've never seen you like this, Alex. You're always the good time, the one who's smiling and having fun."

"Cade tells me this is what love does to a man. I think I can see why I was never in any hurry to fall in love then because I haven't felt good in days."

That makes him throw his head back and laugh. "Your cousin sounds like his father. Love doesn't make men miserable. I've never been unhappy a day since I met your mother. Well, that's not true. There was that time she wouldn't talk to me and I had to camp out in her building's hallway to convince her to take me back after I made a huge mistake. Have you tried doing that?"

"Camping out in Kat's hallway? No. I figured you would have done that thing that actor did in her favorite movie. You know the one with the guy who held up the boom box outside the girl's house."

My father shakes his head. "That's the movies.

People get arrested for doing that kind of thing in real life. That's not really my style either. I like to think I'm smoother than that."

"I don't think she's ever going to forgive me, Dad. I guess I need to accept that and move on like Cade said."

My father's eyebrows slowly rise until they're up into his forehead. "I'm not sure you should be taking advice on love from Cade. He doesn't exactly have a great track record, his current girlfriend excluded."

I stand to leave, knowing I have to get back out to this asinine date. "He's right, though. She's never going to forgive me, so I need to accept that."

He doesn't continue the conversation, which tells me he thinks it's time for me to cut my losses too. Maybe it wasn't love after all. Hell, how would I know? I've never loved anyone in my life.

On my way back to the table, I run into Kane just outside the kitchen entrance. I'm sure my father will clue him in on everything since I know how things work around here, so I give him a nod as I pass and assume he'll head back to the office to find out just what the hell has been going on tonight.

But he grabs my arm before I can walk away, and when I turn to see what's up, he silently waves me into the kitchen. I guess he wants his own personal rundown of the madness of this night.

"What's up, Kane? You can get the details of this shitshow from my father. He'll tell the story better than I even could, I bet."

My uncle shakes his head as I walk with him through the kitchen doors. I follow him to the alcove away from the line and wonder what the hell is going on with him that he wants to talk to me back here.

Leaning in toward me, he whispers low in my ear, "I want you to make sure you don't drink anything at that table when you go back out there. Do you understand me?"

"No. I don't understand. Why can't I drink anything at the table?"

"How well do you know the guy with the camera and the girl?" he asks cryptically, making me even more confused.

"What are you talking about, Kane? This whole thing tonight is pretend. I'm not with her and he's the camera guy from the reality show filming our supposed date. I don't know either of them well at all."

He nods like anything I've said clears things up for him. "Okay. I think one or both of them are trying to sabotage you tonight."

"Why?"

"I saw one of them slip something into your drink. I couldn't tell who did it, but don't drink anything at the table when you get back. In fact, I wouldn't eat anything either."

Staring at him in utter shock, I ask, "Are you serious?"

He frowns at me like he always does when he's unhappy with something here. "Do I look like I'm kidding?"

"No. Okay, thanks. I'm guessing it was Emma. Nothing like slipping a guy a roofie on your fake date."

Then another thought occurs to me. Was she the one who poisoned the chicken dish Kat made? Emma's about the same height with dark hair, so security might have mistakenly thought it was Kat when it was her.

I give Kane's shoulder a thank you pat and head out to the table again. Emma looks upset, which isn't surprising since I've been gone for nearly twenty minutes.

"Where were you? Randy told me you went to some room in the back. Why?"

Good. She doesn't know Kat was here. At least I don't have to explain that.

"Problems with my family. You know how they can get. Just one of the occupational hazards of working with people you're related to. So what did you order me for dessert?"

She presses her lips together, clearly unhappy. "I ordered you what you said to get you, but I had them take it back because it would have been sitting here all this time. Maybe you can get them to bring them out again now that you're back."

At least she didn't spike the dessert. After all that's gone on tonight, I could go for something sweet.

After waving over our server Cherise, I turn my attention back to Emma to see if I can find out if she was the one who poisoned Kat's dish and got her kicked off the show. "Did you enjoy your meal? The risotto is one of our customers' favorites."

Finally, she gives me a smile. "I did. I bet you make a great risotto."

"If I do say so myself, I've been known to. I make a great chicken bourguignon too. That's why I had Kat try to make it last week."

I watch as Emma's smile fades ever so slightly before she forces the corners of her mouth back up into a big smile. "You two were really fighting that day. That must be why she put the poison in it. She thought you'd be eating it the next day."

Shaking my head, I put on my best hurt face. "That's just so hard to believe. I thought we were getting along by the end of the day. We were laughing and joking around. I never thought she'd stay late and put something in the food. I wonder how no one saw her."

Emma quickly fixes my intentionally incorrect statement. "No, she didn't stay late. She went back that night." She stops for a moment and then adds, "She probably knew she couldn't do it if anyone was in the building. That's why she waited until only the security guys were there."

I reach for my glass of water and see Emma's eyes get wide with excitement. "But how did she know when no one would be there? That's what confuses me."

She watches intently as I raise the glass to my lips and then set it back down on the table. Obviously disappointed, she grabs her water glass and raises it into the air to make a toast.

"We should have done this before we ate, but I forgot. Let's toast to a lovely night."

"Sounds good," I say as I raise mine to clink off hers. "To a lovely night with a lovely lady."

Emma eats up the compliment and takes a sip of her water as I slowly move my glass to my mouth again. I have no intention of drinking anything tonight after what Kane told me. Looking around for our server bringing our desserts, I don't see her but I see my uncle standing across the dining room shaking his head.

I didn't forget, for Christ's sake. I just need to find a way to get this water tested to see what she or Randy put in it. Then a thought occurs to me. I'll just take it to the kitchen and put it in a container I know is sterile. We have hundreds of little plastic ramekins for sauces to take out. I can just use one of them.

"Excuse me again. I'm so sorry. I swear my uncle looks like he's having some kind of meltdown over there. I'll be right back. While I'm near the kitchen, I'll check on our desserts."

I hurry away with my water glass before Emma can say a word. As I pass Kane on my way into the kitchen, he chuckles. "Planning on giving that to someone you don't like?"

"No. I'm planning to get it tested to find out what the hell she put in my drink. I'm assuming she roofied it, but I want to get proof because I don't think this is the first time she's poisoned something. Last time it was food, though."

I quickly find a ramekin and pour the water into it before walking back out to where Kane stands watching Emma and the table like a hawk. Handing him the container, I say, "I want you to put this in the office. I'll get it tomorrow."

He gives me a grin and walks away with what I'm hoping will be my proof that Emma's the one who should be thrown off the reality show, not Kat. When I get back to the table with my new glass with fresh water, Cherise has just arrived with our desserts, thankfully. At least I can enjoy my chocolate cake without wondering if it's been spiked.

"Sorry about that." I tap the rim of my glass off hers and flash Emma a big smile. "To a lovely lady."

She watches with wide eyes as I lift the glass to my lips and take a big drink of water. I'm barely able to contain my smile at her excitement that she thinks she just drugged me.

"I'm not really feeling like dessert right now. At least not this one," she says with a giggle. "What do you say we have the server box these up and we can leave?"

I know what she's doing. Roofies take effect pretty quickly, so she has less than a half hour to get me out of this restaurant before I start acting strange. Since two of my family members are nearby, she has to make sure we're away from here if she's going to get to take advantage of my impaired state.

She's going to be disappointed when I don't get confused and unable to function. That she thinks this is the way to get with a man amazes me. We're usually pretty easy. You don't have to drug us. You just have to offer us something we want.

Too bad for Emma that the only woman I want is Kat.

I wink and wave the server over to take care of our desserts as Emma stands to leave. "Someone's in a big hurry," I say jokingly.

Emma gives me a flirty smile before grabbing her purse. "I'll be right back. I just want to visit the ladies' room before we leave."

Flashing her a big smile, I nod and then look over at Randy filming all of this. The son of a bitch probably knows exactly what Emma's got planned and intends on getting every sick minute of it.

Into the camera, I say, "Who needs desserts when we have the rest of the night?"

Randy chuckles, the asshole. Sick fuck. Who thinks recording someone taking advantage of a person who's been drugged is cool? The two of them are fucked up.

When Emma returns, I notice she's fixed her makeup and lipstick. Nice that she bothered to get pretty to date rape me. Too bad she's going to be disappointed.

"Ready?" she says eagerly.

Again, into the camera, I say, "I was born ready."

I stand up to leave and think to myself I've finally found a way to be comfortable with being filmed constantly. It helps that I'm wise to what the two of them have planned.

We all pile into the limo, with Randy sitting in the back with us this time since he says he needs to make sure he gets every great moment, and as we wind through the streets of Tampa, I feel like an animal at the zoo with the way they're watching me. By the time we reach Emma's house, I'm still fully in control of my faculties, something that shocks both of them.

I quickly exit the limo and walk around to open her door, deciding that being a gentleman to my intended rapist is the best way to play this. She stares up at me in utter confusion as I escort her out of the car and up the sidewalk to her house.

"That was a nice time," I say with a smile she should be sensing is far too smug right now. "I'm sorry about the craziness with my family, but they come with me as a package. See you at the studio tomorrow."

Emma says nothing, no doubt stunned I'm still upright, as she stands holding her dessert box. When I lean down to give her a kiss, I see Randy a few feet away filming. He likely can't understand why I'm not laid out in the back of the limo either.

"Good night, Emma."

And with that, I walk down the sidewalk and pass Randy who's no longer holding the camera up to do his job. "Let's go. I need to get home."

I consider saying something to him about whatever she put into my drink, but I decide to wait until I find out what it is. Better to have all the facts before I go to Maria and Shane.

Then they can know Kat wasn't the person who poisoned Murphy. Emma did.

CHAPTER TWELVE

at

I RUN PAST SADIE SITTING ON THE LIVING ROOM couch when I get home from CK, throwing myself into bed to cry myself to sleep after all that happened. No matter how much I want Alex, I can't forgive him or forget what he did.

Even as I wish I could more than he will ever know.

"Where have you been?" she asks and then sits on the bed next to me.

Into the pillow, I say, "I went to CK. You know, the place where Alex works."

"Whatever for?" Sadie asks in a voice filled with shock. Or maybe it's horror. Whatever it is, she sounds like she wants to shake me by the shoulders and hopes it helps get some sense into me.

Turning my head to look at her, I wipe my eyes and admit the truth. "I don't know. Or I do and it's so damn sad I hate to admit it."

"Were you hoping he'd be there?"

"I don't know. Maybe. Or maybe I just wanted to be there where he works. I'm a pathetic mess."

Sadie gently pats my arm and tries to comfort me. "Well, I'm guessing something happened by the way you're acting. Did you see him?"

I nod, almost too humiliated to admit what happened to her. "He was on a date with that Emma girl from the show. He looked so happy, Sadie. I swear, he looked like he did when he and I…"

The words get stuck in my throat. Spent the night together. How could I have been so stupid?

"Was it for the show? Like one of those reality TV dates? Because if it was, then he had to pretend he was having a good time. You know how that works," she says, trying too hard to make me feel better.

"I know," I sulk. "I know it wasn't real. He told me it wasn't. It's just that he looked so happy, and it was all pretend. Was it all pretend with me because he just wanted to sleep with me?"

My best friend smiles like I'm the biggest fool in the world. "Honey, can I give you a little tough love? No man in the world would pretend to be happy just to sleep with you. You make it far too hard for any of them and getting sex from you wouldn't be worth it for all they'd have to do."

Damn, that is tough love.

"Wow, that came out pretty harsh. Did you mean it to be that cruel?" I ask with a sniffle.

She shrugs like she isn't sorry, even though I know she cares about me. "It is what it is, Kat. You're a lot of work, but you're the kind of girlfriend most guys would kill for once they grow up. You just happen to date men who are oversized children."

A lot of work. Well, she's not wrong there. All those defensive walls I've built up exist for a good reason, after all.

Then what Heidi told me at work comes rushing back into my brain, and for the first time since I heard the news about Rafe's impending marriage, I cry. As I sob into the pillow, Sadie rubs my back.

"I wasn't trying to hurt your feelings. I'm sorry."

Wiping my eyes, I shake my head at her mistake and sniffle again. "I'm not crying because of that. I'm crying because I heard Rafe is getting married to that homewrecker he cheated on me with. On top of everything else, the guy I thought I was going to spend the rest of my life with is going to walk down the aisle to spend the rest of his life with her."

"Aw, honey. I'm sorry. I wouldn't have said all those things if I knew."

Tired of crying and feeling bad, I sit up and dry my eyes. "It's okay. You said what you believe. You aren't wrong. I've got walls. I admit it. A good couple feet of them are because of that bastard Rafe and what he did."

Sadie gives me a sympathetic smile before hugging me. "You know, I was thinking you haven't felt this bad since all that happened with him. You must really care about Alex March."

"I do, but how is that possible? We only slept together once, and while I admit he was great in bed, it was only one time. On top of that, we've only known each other for like a week. Who falls for someone that fast? Not me, for sure, but here I am all weepy over him for days on end."

My roommate shakes her head and smiles. "Honey, you've known Alex March for ages. That first night when you and your parents went to CK and he came out to the table after your father asked to talk to the chef you came back here and he was all you could talk about. I think a lot of what's going on with all this crying has to do with being thrown off the show and you blaming him because what he did only reinforces the idea you had about him from that first night—that he's one of those people who always get the applause while you get to toil outside the limelight."

I stare at her in disbelief even as I have to accept she's probably right. "That sounds pretty screwed up. You really must think I'm a headcase."

With a big smile, she says, "I told you. I'm not the only one with daddy issues."

And right there in my tiny bedroom in the average apartment I share with my best friend, it all becomes clear. "This isn't all about Alex. This is about my father too. Jesus, I am a fucking mess."

"Of course it is! How could it not be? You do the same job as your father has all his adult life, and all you've ever wanted was his approval. Then he goes and gives it to a man who is just like him. I mean, look at the two of them. Both are charming, both get kudos for their work, and both have no idea how easy their lives have been compared to yours. And you know what the worst part of all of this is?"

Oh, God. There's an even worse part than my being an emotional mess with daddy issues?

"No."

"I doubt either one of them have a clue how much just being themselves makes you feel like you're nothing special."

And that is worse.

Feeling like total shit, I collapse back onto the bed and pull the pillow over my head. "I think I'm going to spend the rest of my life here. Make sure to tell anyone who comes to see me that it's all over. I'll be staying in bed until I shake off this mortal coil."

"Oh, more Shakespeare! That must mean you're feeling a little better already."

"No, I'm not," I answer into the pillow.

"Well, you will. As soon as your parents leave after their visit."

And the hits just keep on coming.

I toss away the pillow and look over at Sadie as she nods in sympathy for me. "In all of this craziness, I forgot about my mother and father coming here tomorrow. She said she wanted to make reservations at CK, and there's no way I'm going to be able to get out of going to dinner with them. God, I hope he isn't there then. I just want to forget about Alex March. Is it too much to ask for this one good thing to happen to me? Maybe if I ask my mother to make the reservations as early as possible I can escape running into him because he'll still be at the studio with the show."

As she stands up from the bed, Sadie chuckles. "That's the spirit! Avoidance. I'm going to get something to eat since all this talk of restaurants and chefs has made me hungry. You want anything, or are you keeping with your plan to stay in bed?"

"No, I'm not hungry, but for future reference, I'd like to point out that staying in bed is not synonymous with a hunger strike. Food can be brought in here."

Sadie walks out of my bedroom, calling back as she heads toward the kitchen, "I'll keep that in mind!"

I take a deep breath and let our conversation rattle around in my head. I definitely have daddy issues, but I didn't realize they were so deep with my father and Alex so interconnected in my mind. Sadie's right about that.

But what do I do now that I know? Or is it too

late? Have I pushed him away too many times for us to have any chance at all?

A NOISE OUT IN THE LIVING ROOM ROUSES ME FROM my sleep, and I grab my phone off the nightstand to see the time. 8:55. Sadie should be at work by now, so who's making the racket?

Rubbing the sleep from my eyes, I stumble out into the hallway and instantly know my parents have arrived by the scent of my mother's Chanel perfume wafting through the air. Why didn't she mention they were getting a flight out at the crack of dawn today?

Quickly, I run my hands through my mess of hair and glance down my body to make sure I look presentable. Well, not presentable but at least clothed. My mother will no doubt be appalled by my appearance since she's never looked disheveled a day in her life.

With all my body parts covered, I paste a smile onto my face and walk into the living room. My mother takes one look at me, and her eyes nearly bug out of her head.

"Oh, Katerina. Did we wake you?" she asks, likely hoping to God I don't look like this at any other time than when I'm sleeping.

"It's okay, Mom. I would have been up and waiting for you, but you didn't say you were getting here so early."

She opens her arms wide, showing off her thin frame clothed in a navy-blue designer dress under her white sweater. "Give me a hug. It's so good to see you, honey."

My nose fills with her perfume as she hugs me to her, and the delicate scent brings back memories of all the good times we've had together. "It's good to see you too, Mom."

I step back and turn to look at my father. "It's good to see you too, Dad."

Dressed in a pair of black dress pants and a teal blue button-down shirt that accentuates his dark hair and green eyes, my father relaxes on the couch with his arms spread wide on the back of the cushion. He looks utterly confident, like always, and even though he likely wouldn't be caught dead in a place like this if I didn't live here, Andrew Truesdale looks like he's a king on his throne ruling over his kingdom.

"You should live in a better place, Katerina," he says with a hint of disgust in his voice as he looks around at my apartment.

That's what he says every time he comes here. I'd live in a better place if I could afford it, but since that lovely bitch Deidre just decreased my pay by two dollars an hour, I'll be lucky if I can swing rent here without picking up hours at another job.

I don't want to think about that today, though, so I simply smile and make a joke about all the good places being taken in Tampa. He narrows his eyes at my lame attempt at humor, like he can't imagine how we could be related since I'm nowhere as self-assured as he always is.

My mother takes a seat next to him and asks, "Honey, why are your eyes all red?"

Since I don't want to say anything about crying most of the night, I shrug and play it off with a lie. "I think it's allergies. Pollen. It gets pretty bad down here."

"You never had allergies when you lived in New York. I swear you'd do better if you lived up there again," she says, ending her claim with a heavy sigh.

The last thing I want to do is get into a discussion about how I should move back up north, so I change the subject, hoping to put the focus on them instead of me. "So why did you guys come to visit?"

For the first time since I walked into the living room, my father smiles. "I have big news. I'm retiring. Of course, you'll be expected to attend my retirement party, Katerina."

As if I can afford airfare to New York on my recently reduced salary. I don't want to talk about that, though, so I simply nod and say, "I wouldn't miss it for the world, Dad. Congratulations! Retirement is a big deal. Are you looking forward to being able to do what you want every day of the week?"

He doesn't answer, but his less than thrilled expression tells me he isn't. If that's the case, why is he retiring?

And then my mother speaks up, and I know the answer to that question.

"And we have another piece of good news, honey. We're going to sell the house and move down here to be close to you. Isn't that wonderful?"

I feel my mouth drop open as shock rushes through me. Move down here to be close to me? Why? I'm twenty-five years old. I don't need my parents to be hanging around all the time, which is what will happen if they move here.

"Here? Really? I didn't think you liked Florida, Mom. You always say the heat is oppressive, and Dad, what will you do with all your new time off without the city nearby to entertain you?" I ask, my voice verging on panic.

"You have a city right here."

"Yes, but Tampa isn't like New York. That's the greatest city in the world. You always say that. Ever since I was a little girl, you've said New York is the greatest city in the world. There's Broadway and Little Italy and Chinatown and Chelsea. I mean, I don't think I've seen more than one or two art galleries the entire time I've lived here."

My father gives me a strange look, as if he understands the last thing I want in my life is to have my parents living right nearby. My mother, though, remains blissfully ignorant to my fear that they'll go through with moving down here.

"Everywhere has air conditioning, so it'll fine," she

says, dashing my hopes that the Florida heat would keep her nearly a thousand miles away. "My friend Monica thought she'd hate it, but when she moved down here to live with her daughter and son-in-law after they had their baby, she told me she grew to love it. She says I'll forget all about New York in a New York minute."

Fantastic. I think I need a drink. Is nine in the morning too early to get drunk to forget about your life?

Standing up abruptly from the couch, my father announces they're going house hunting. "So get ready. We want you with us because we don't know a thing about the area."

"Dad, I have work," I say, even though I'm not scheduled for hours.

That excuse doesn't deter him. Waving his hand like he's making magic, he says, "Call off. This is important. It's not like you see your parents every day."

Except I will if they move down here.

"I can't. I took off all last week for that reality show."

God, I hate saying that.

My father huffs his disgust. "Well, that was a waste of your time."

His utter disapproval hurts like getting smacked across the face. "Why? Because I'm not good enough to compete against great chefs?"

Shaking his head, he grumbles, "Because it's beneath you. You're a Truesdale."

Unsure what he means, I say, "Well, it wasn't beneath Alex March, the head chef at CK. He's one of the competitors."

My father's face contorts into an expression of revulsion, and his eyes open wide in shock. "It's beneath him too. What is wrong with this part of the country? Do people here not understand chefs of your caliber and his don't belong on some silly reality show?"

I stand there in stunned silence as his words sink in. He just said I was as good a chef as the one he raved about. Chefs of our caliber.

This time, I don't try to stop the tears as they overtake me. "You've never said anything that nice about my abilities as a chef, Daddy."

"I assumed you knew. Why would I always tell you how you should quit that job of yours?" he says matter-of-factly.

As I wipe my eyes, I smile. "I thought you said that because it isn't a four-star restaurant."

"I say that because that place isn't good enough for my daughter to work in."

Sniffling as my happy tears subside, I say, "Well, then I guess I shouldn't tell you that Deidre demoted me to salad prep because I got thrown off that reality show."

My mother grabs my father's hand to stop him, but

it's no use. He storms away, waving his hands as he barks, "You should quit just for that alone. You're far too talented to be a salad prep, Katerina. You're a Truesdale, for God's sake! I swear this is because you're a woman. Your grandfather and I never got demoted or passed over at any restaurant."

"Maybe I'm just not as good as you and Grandpa," I quietly say, hating that it could be the real reason for my demotion.

But my father dismisses that notion with another wave of his hand. "Nonsense! No daughter of mine could ever be anything less than a first-class chef. You shouldn't take her treatment of you, Katerina. You deserve so much better than her and that place."

As he stomps around complaining about Frederick's and my mother tries to get him to calm down, warning him about his blood pressure and how this trip is supposed to be all about relaxing, all I can do is smile. My father has never said anything like that to me.

And I've never felt more wonderful in my life than I do at this moment.

CHAPTER THIRTEEN

lex

My legs stretched out in front of me and my feet resting on the coffee table, I lean back against the sofa and close my eyes after another long and frustrating day on that damn reality show. We tape a show a day, so all I can hope is they aren't planning on having this thing run longer than eight or ten shows. With any luck, I'll be back in my own kitchen by the end of next week.

I just want to forget this whole thing. The show. Emma trying to roofie me on our pretend date. All the bullshit that involves so little of doing what I love most —cooking.

And Kat. I have to accept she's never going to

forgive me. I fucked up. Now I know what it feels like to truly want someone in your life and not be able to have that one wish come true.

Jesus, if this is love, it sucks. Why the hell would anyone want to feel this? I think I preferred when I was a hedonistic manwhore who enjoyed his life.

I blow the air out of my lungs. No, I didn't. It's true I had fun. That was it, though. Nothing ever became permanent. I thought for a long time that's what I wanted out of life. Good times every night with a different woman. I mean, who would say no to that?

Then Meadow came along, and I realized I liked the idea of being with one person. That ended, though, and I figured while everyone else in my world found that special someone, that wasn't meant to be for me.

Until Kat.

We made the oddest pair. I'm happy-go-lucky and love my life, and that woman is infuriatingly defensive. At least that's what I thought at first. Once I got to know her, though, I saw she's different when she isn't busy propping up her walls so no one can possibly get close to her.

I thought I met the one when we finally got together. Beautiful, sexy, and as passionate about cooking as I am, I wanted to believe we could be happy.

And then I fucked it all up.

Grabbing the remote, I turn on the TV to give me

something to think about other than Kat. Some baseball game is on, but I'm not in the mood to care about who's playing or who's winning. It's meant to be background noise I can focus on every time she pops into my head.

My phone vibrates across the coffee table, and I see it's my father calling. He probably wants to know what happened after Emma and I left the restaurant last night. If Kane told him about her putting something in my drink, he's probably worried I may have been drugged, so I guess I should answer.

Reluctantly, I lean over and grab my phone. "Hey, Dad. What's up?"

"Alex, I just saw that woman who was in my office with you last night sit down at a table with two people I'm thinking are her parents. I thought you might like to know."

As if someone turned the page on my life, I suddenly see a chance to show Kat I care about her. Standing up, I begin to hurry around my place as my father asks how things turned out last night.

"It wasn't like it was a real date, Dad, so it turned out as well as can be expected. I grabbed the water Kane thinks she drugged early this morning before I went to the taping for the show, so I'm hoping to find out in a few days just what the hell she tried to dose me with. I can't really talk right now, though. I need to get ready."

The smile in my father's voice comes through loud

and clear as he says, "You're coming over? Good. Do you want me to do anything?"

I grab my black dress pants and stick one leg in while I balance on one foot and hold the phone to my ear. "No, just keep them there for a little while. It's going to take me a couple minutes to get dressed and drive over there."

"No problem. They just sat down, so even assuming they got our normal service, they'll be here for at least an hour. I can tell the kitchen to hold things up, if you want."

As I slide my other leg into my pants and button them, I have to laugh. "I had no idea you were such a matchmaker, Dad. I thought you left that kind of thing to Mom."

"I do what I can when I get the chance. I'm looking out into the dining room right now. We're getting pretty busy, so I might not have to do anything to keep them here. Just get over here as fast as you can."

Heading to my closet to find a dress shirt, I smile at how funny he can be about things sometimes. "Ok, thanks, Dad. See you in a little while."

"Good luck, son."

I toss my phone onto the bed and turn to face the clothes I have to choose from. The gray shirt will work. I should probably wear a tie too since that's the dress code at CK. The black and red diamond pattern one will work.

Five minutes and the world's fastest Windsor knot and teeth brushing later, I'm racing downstairs to my car. If there's little traffic, I can probably get there by the time their entrées arrive at their table. Not exactly my best timing, but I have to take my chances when they come.

My father and Kane are waiting just inside the dining room when I arrive. Both smiling, they look me up and down like they're the style police.

"Looking good. You must really like this one," Kane says with a chuckle.

I don't bother answering him before my father reaches out and brushes a piece of lint off my shoulder. "They ordered the steak and prosciutto skewers for an appetizer, so that bought you a little time."

"Okay, wish me luck."

Both men give me a pat on the back to send me off, and with a deep breath, I begin to walk toward Kat's table. I just need to be casual, and hopefully, she won't try to gouge my eyes out with a skewer.

Her father spies me first and gives me a welcoming smile. That's a good sign. At least one person at the table doesn't hate me.

"Kat, I'm so happy to see you here tonight," I say.

She turns to look up at me, and for a moment, it seems like she isn't sure how to react. She quickly forces a smile and extends her hand to shake mine, as if we're some kind of business associates who met a few times at a company meeting or something.

"Hi, Alex. It's nice to see you."

Not a bad beginning. It could have been a little better, but I don't have a skewer jutting out from my eye socket, so I'm thankful for that.

"Mom and Dad, this is Alex March, the head chef here at CK. You met him once before when we dined here," she says to her parents, and I see a look of recognition on both their faces as they smile politely at me.

"You don't look like you're working tonight," her mother says.

"No, I have some time off because of another project I'm involved in, but since my family runs the restaurant, I'm here a lot anyway."

Her father looks up at me, twisting his expression into one of disgust exactly like I've seen so often from his daughter. "Are you referring to that reality show you and my daughter were on?"

Clearly, he doesn't think much of Chef on Chef. Then again, it isn't surprising since his daughter was thrown off the show.

I nod, hoping his mention of the damn reality show hasn't soured any chances I have to get Kat to talk to me. Eager to change the subject, I look at the appetizer in the middle of the table and say, "I love the steak and prosciutto skewers. I think I ate about a hundred of them before we first introduced them. I felt like I had an obligation to be a taste tester before we offered them to our customers."

That makes her father's face light up. "I've been known to do that too when my restaurants are introducing a new menu item." Patting his non-existent belly, he laughs. "More than once my pants didn't fit after all my taste testing."

As we talk about eating too much in our attempts to make sure what we offer is the best it can be, Kat stares at me and I notice her eyes aren't filled with hate or revulsion. Maybe she'll be open to talking after they're finished with their meal.

"Well, I just wanted to come over and say hello. It was nice seeing you again, Mr. and Mrs. Truesdale. And Kat, it's great to see you too. Please let me know if you need anything tonight. I'll be happy to get you whatever you want."

As I give them one final smile before leaving, her father motions to the other side of the table next to his daughter and says, "Since you aren't working, please join us."

I quickly glance at his wife, who looks thrilled by his suggestion, and then his daughter, and I'm happy to see she looks pleased to have me join them too. I hadn't planned on crashing their night out, but if this lets me have a chance to show Kat that I want to make up for what I did, then I can't say no.

"I'd be happy to. Thank you."

Out of the corner of my eye, I see my father

practically jumping for joy on the other side of the dining room. He really is an old romantic soul, after all.

As the meal progresses, her father and I talk about what he calls the silly reality show, and I can't disagree with anything he has to say about it. I can tell Kat is uncomfortable about the subject, so I take the opportunity to change the subject to something about him whenever he brings up Chef on Chef.

By the time the meal is over, it's clear her father is definitely a fan of mine, and her mother seems to like me too. Kat, on the other hand, has gradually moved from happy to see me to what appears to be eager to leave. I've tried my best to impress her parents, and it seems to have worked.

Now if I could only get their daughter to think as well of me.

"Thank you, Alex. This has been such a wonderful time. Your chefs did a superb job on everything. I loved the taste of my lamb," Mrs. Truesdale says.

"I'm so happy you enjoyed it. That's what we strive for here at CK." I know I sound like a total company man, but it's the truth. "I care about the food our customers are served, and all my chefs care too. It's what makes this restaurant such an incredible place to work."

When her father reaches for the bill, I shake my head and smile. "Please, this is on me. It's been a wonderful time. Thank you for offering me the chance to get to know you."

That impresses him even more, which is exactly what I intended. The parents seem covered, but once glance at Kat's painful, forced smile tells me I have a lot more work to do.

As they stand to leave, I lean over and say to her, "Can we talk?"

She shakes her head and frowns. "No, I can't. Sorry."

"Alex, we need to get back to the hotel. It's been a very long day, and I need to relax. Would you be able to give Katerina a ride to her apartment? It would help us out because that's all the way across town and our hotel is just a block away from here," her mother says sweetly, clearly picking up on her daughter's emotions.

Standing from the table, I say, "I'm happy to. Go have a relaxing night, and I'll make sure Kat gets home safe and sound."

"Great! Thank you. Her father and I appreciate it."

After we all say goodbye, I think I'll have a chance to talk to Kat now that she's alone, but not a minute after her parents walk out of the restaurant, she storms toward the door. Not willing to let this opportunity slip out of my hands, I run out after her.

She's marching through the parking lot by the time I get outside, so I sprint to catch up with her, barely reaching her before she makes it to the road. "Kat, wait! I just want to talk."

Spinning around to face me, she snaps, "My mother thinks she's helping me. She doesn't know that entire thing you did in there at dinner was an act. I want nothing to do with you."

"It wasn't an act. I had a good time with your parents. Your father and I got along famously. I could talk to him about kitchens and his career as a chef for hours. It wasn't an act at all."

Every word seems to anger her more, and she storms away again without saying another thing. I catch up to her quickly this time and grab her arm to hold her there before she bolts out into traffic.

"Please, listen to me! Why are you so angry at me tonight? What did I do at dinner to make you this unhappy? And don't say it was all an act because you know it wasn't."

She stares up at me with so much anger that I almost expect her to reach out and slap me across the face, but slowly, that rage inside her fades away. Her shoulders sag, and she lets out a heavy sigh, like she's been carrying the weight of the world and finally just wants to let it go.

"You have no idea how you make me feel when I'm near you and you're so confident and comfortable with someone like my father, Alex. All my life I've wanted to be like that. Like you. Instead, I'm me, and it never feels like it's enough. That entire meal I felt like I faded away into the woodwork once you and he got talking."

A car drives into the parking lot, so I gently guide her down the sidewalk toward the park nearby. "I'm sorry. I didn't mean to do that. That wasn't my intention. I was honestly just trying to impress your parents because I care about you, and from all I've ever heard, if her parents don't like you, that's a problem."

In the moonlight, she looks so fragile and beautiful that I want to take her into my arms and hold her until she doesn't feel like this anymore. I had no idea I was making her so unhappy all that time.

"Do you know what my father said to me today?" she says in a small voice as we slowly walk together.

I don't answer her question because I don't want to make things worse. Instead, I wait for her to continue.

She lets out another heavy sigh and says, "He told me that the reality show wasn't for people like you or me because of our caliber. For the first time in my life, he said something about my abilities as a chef that showed me he thinks I'm talented. Do you know how I know that?"

I shake my head, but I have an idea why.

"Because he compared me to someone like you. I took that compliment, though, because it meant the world to me."

I step in front of her and stop her with my hands on her shoulders. "You are talented, and you don't have to be lumped in with me to be that. You're talented all on your own, Kat. I wish you believed that like I do."

She gives me a tiny smile to go with her teary eyes. "Was it just coincidence that you were at the restaurant tonight? I would have thought you'd be exhausted after a long day at the studio."

Smiling, I shake my head. "No. My father called me to let me know you were here. I hurried and got dressed to get here as soon as I could because I was hoping to have a chance to talk to you."

"You came here for me?"

"Of course. I want to prove to you I'm sorry for what I did. I keep trying and failing, but I figure one of these times I'm going to say the right thing and then you won't hate me anymore."

Kat wipes the tears from under her eyes and sighs. "I don't hate you, Alex."

"Well, that's progress."

"You don't want to be with someone like me. Trust me on that. I'm a mess. I mean, that you can't see that tells me you're either blind or willfully ignorant, but I am."

I tuck her hair behind her ear and slide my finger along her jaw to tilt her chin up so she has to look at me when I say, "I don't think you're a mess. I think you're beautiful and talented and someone I want to spend time with."

"Even after all the things I said to you? Why?"

She seems to think I need a better excuse than her being beautiful and talented. So I give her another reason, the one reason that means more to me than any other.

"I've never met anyone who challenges me like you do. And not just because you make me climb over those walls you've built up around you. You're as good a chef as I am, maybe better because you've had to fight to be recognized, and I love being around you because of that. No other woman I've ever been with has ever shared that passion I have for cooking. I'm not sure I knew it, but I've wanted to meet someone like you for so long, and now that I have, I'm not letting you go without a fight, Kat Truesdale."

"Even though I'm a fucked-up mess with daddy issues that keep getting in our way?"

I smile at her attempt to make me think she isn't the most incredible woman I've ever met. "We'll work on that. If you're willing, I am. What do you say? Will you give me another chance?"

Kat nods and throws her arms around me. "I'm so sorry I've been so difficult, Alex. I don't mean to be like this. I guess I've been working hard on those walls around me."

As I press a kiss to the top of her head, she sighs against me, and I feel like what just happened changed everything between us.

CHAPTER FOURTEEN

at

WE WALK INTO HIS CONDO, AND IT FEELS DIFFERENT this time. I feel different. Something about admitting how messed up I am and not having him run away makes me want to believe this thing between us can happen.

I want it to. After all the time I've spent trying to hate Alex March, I think it might be time to give another emotion a chance. Maybe even love.

He holds my hand as he leads me to his bedroom, and I love how strong and protective his hand feels against my skin. Since Rafe, I've worked hard to make sure I don't need or even want that kind of strength in any man.

Tonight, I want to admit to myself I crave that in my life.

"Do you want anything to eat?" he asks, almost as an afterthought, like he realized we're almost to his bed and he hasn't even offered me anything before we get naked. "I could make you something small, in case you're hungry since you didn't have dessert at dinner."

His dark eyes seem to dance in the dim light from the sconce on the wall as we walk past it. He is the most beautiful creature I've ever seen, and right now as he's trying to be sweet and thoughtful, I know why so many women want him.

"I'm not hungry. For food, at least," I say with a big smile, happy to let him know how much I look forward to us being together.

"Okay," he says with a chuckle. "Just let me know if I can get you anything."

I tug on his hand to stop him, and when he turns to face me, I lift myself up on my toes to take the first thing I want from him. Pressing a kiss to his lips, I savor the sweetness of desire on them.

"That's one thing I was hungry for," I say against them, loving their softness.

"I've got more of that. Feel free to take all you want."

I let my hands drift down over his chest and bite my lip in anticipation of him naked beneath me in a few seconds. "Be careful. I'll take you up on that offer."

Alex stuffs his hand into my hair and tugs my head back so tingles of pain race across my scalp. Brushing his lips against mine, he whispers, "Good. I want you to."

Lifting me off the floor, he brings me up to waist level, and I wrap my legs around his body. God, I've missed him! His hands slide beneath my ass, and his cock presses against the front of my damp panties. Thick and long and hard, just the feel of him against my needy clit makes me wish I hadn't worn anything under my dress.

"Rip them off if you want. Just hurry," I say, practically breathlessly, dying to finally feel him slide inside me.

His fingers play with the fabric for a moment before he simply tears them in half and rips them down my left leg. A second later, he thrusts into me in one hard push that fills me completely.

In his ear, I moan as my mind fills with only one thing. Alex. "Oh, God..."

"You feel so fucking good," he groans as he begins to thrust his hips, sliding his cock out of me and then ramming it back inside until there's nothing left separating our bodies.

My hands cling to his neck as we fuck, the two of us finding our rhythm just as we did that first night we were together. It's as incredible as that time, but now, we have lost time to make up for.

"I missed you so much," I whisper as my hands

tear at his shirt. Still dressed, he smiles as I struggle to get to his skin. I want to feel him.

He's powerful against me, and with each time he strokes into my body, I feel like I'm melting inside. All the anger and resentment I've kept inside me for so long, not only for him but for so many other things in my life, disappears as I surrender everything I am to him.

I yearn for his body and desperately run my hands up over his chest, loving the feel of his smooth tanned skin against my fingertips. Every desire I've secretly harbored as I protested how much I hated him comes alive here in his arms, and as he pushes his hips forward and thrusts his cock back into me, I feel like I'm burning up.

Alex kisses me long and deep, and I sense us moving across the room. I open my eyes as he lowers me to the bed, leaving my body empty and me wishing he'd return to me.

He gives me one of his sexy smiles as he shrugs out of his shirt and strips his pants off. Sliding up my body, he cradles my face and drags his thumb over my mouth before he kisses me long and deep, his tongue teasing mine as he pushes into my pussy.

"I promised myself if I ever got the chance to have this happen again, I'd make sure you knew how much I missed you, Kat," he says with a moan, pressing his forehead to mine and staring down at me with a look full of need in his dark eyes.

The feel of his cock touching a spot deep inside me makes it difficult not to let my eyes roll back into my head, but I want to watch this and remember the very moment I let him into my soul. I was so stupid for so long. I don't want to feel that way anymore.

The corded muscles in his neck strain against his skin with every push of his hips. His intensity captivates me, taking me with him as we race toward our release. My heels at the base of his spine push hard into his sweat drenched back. We're close to that perfect moment we both so desperately crave, and when he begins making shallow stabs into me instead of the smooth thrusts he'd begun with, I sense he's almost there.

I want this, the sensual moments that are the very essence of Alex. Clinging to his shoulders, I say practically sobbing, "Don't stop."

He looks down at me, his eyes narrowed as he winces slightly, and I feel the first tendrils of my orgasm unspool inside me. Raking my fingernails down his back, I cry out as my release washes over me like a tidal wave of emotion and sensation.

With one final thrust, Alex stills inside me, every muscle in his body stiffening as he floods my insides. Completely satisfied, we both let out heavy sighs as we lay there panting as sweat covers our skin.

For the first time with any man, I feel like I'm safe. I feel like I'm home.

CHAPTER FIFTEEN

lex

I DON'T ROLL OFF HER AFTER WE BOTH COME, HAPPY to watch her as she recovers from her orgasm. She's beautiful and all I've been able to think about the entire time she was gone from my life. I don't want to be without her ever again.

This feels so foreign yet so natural to me. I don't know if I ever thought I'd find the one, that mythical woman who I'd want to spend the rest of my life with. Then Kat showed up, and as much as I wanted to feel anything but love for her, she wove herself into the fabric of my life, and when she was gone from it, I missed her so much I didn't know if I'd ever be the same again.

I'd finally found the one.

"Is everything okay?" she asks with more than a hint of concern in her voice. "Alex?"

I drop my head to press a kiss to her lips and nod. "Everything's great."

Now could be the moment I tell her how I feel. The thing is I've never said those three words to any woman. I never felt them before. So maybe now isn't the right time to say them.

I'm not sure. All I'm sure about is I missed Kat far too much for her to be just another woman I spend time with. She's so much more than that.

"So now that we've made up, can I ask you a question?" she says quietly.

Rolling off her, I prop my head up on my hand and smile. "Sure. Anything. Shoot."

"Were you miserable these last few days?"

Her eyes are filled with curiosity, so I quickly answer with a nod and say, "I was. I don't think I've ever been more miserable than I felt from the moment you drove out of the studio parking lot that day."

Kat gently caresses my cheek before giving me a kiss. "I didn't want you miserable. I never wanted that. I guess I was just wondering because I was miserable too."

"Yeah, but you were unhappy because I let you down. I was unhappy because you weren't in my life anymore."

She shakes her head and sighs. "I thought that too,

but when I saw you tonight at the restaurant, I knew I'd been so miserable because you weren't around anymore. When you came over to the table, I felt like someone had lifted a fifty-pound weight off my chest."

"Two miserable peas in a pod. That's another thing we have in common."

My sad little joke makes her laugh, and I watch her like I've never looked at anyone else in my entire life. It's like making her happy makes me happy. It's always been that way with sex for me, but now it's like just seeing Kat laugh makes my heart fill with joy.

"I don't think you were ever miserable. It's not in your nature, Alex. You're a happy-go-lucky guy. Me? Misery seems to be my best friend, even if I'm not interested in being hers."

Pulling her to me, I wrap my arms around her in a hug. "Whatever I was, it was because you weren't in my life anymore and I knew you hated me. I never want to feel that way again."

She kisses my ear, and shaking her head, says, "I never hated you. Not really."

I roll over onto my back, taking her with me so she's straddling my hips on top of me. "Well, I deserved it if you did, so it's okay."

Kat looks away, unwilling to face me, and sighs. "It was never hate. I wish it was. But it wasn't. It was jealousy. Sadie made me realize that."

Sliding my hands down her sides, I let them come

to rest on her hips. "You have nothing to be jealous of. You're every bit the chef I am, Kat."

She waves away my compliment, but I see in her smile she loves hearing that. It's true. She is as talented a chef as I am, maybe even more.

"It had to do with my father, which is something I don't want to talk about while we're both naked and I'm sitting on top of you as your hard cock presses against my ass," she says with a chuckle. "But Sadie helped me see the light. And here I thought she was the queen of daddy issues."

I pull her down to kiss that beautiful mouth of hers and joke, "Now we're getting into an area that has to do with my uncle, and I'm right there with you not wanting to talk about him while all my body can think of is how much I want to be inside you again."

"Then I think we need to stop talking and get to more enjoyable things, like make up sex."

Kat lifts herself up and a second later I watch her lower herself down onto me, my cock filling her completely. "That's a good first step, don't you think?" she asks with a grin.

"It is."

Before she can start riding me, I roll the two of us over so she's on her back. Her expression and wide eyes tell me she's surprised.

As I slide my hands down to her knees to lift her legs, I explain, "I felt like I should be the one doing more of the work tonight in our make up sex since I was the one in the wrong."

She seems to think about it for a moment before smiling up at me. "I'm all for you being in charge, but you don't have to work for my forgiveness anymore, Alex. Trust me. I'm here naked in your bed. I definitely forgive you."

The head of my cock slides into her wet pussy, and inch by inch I fill her until our bodies meld into one. She's tight and hot, and it takes every bit of willpower I possess not to simply fuck like I always have.

But Kat isn't a woman like all the rest.

Her hands cling to the back of my neck, pulling me to her, and I kiss her long and deep like everything I've ever needed exists in her beautiful mouth. Slowly, I slide my cock out of her snug cunt and then even slower I ease back inside her body. I want this to last to show her how happy I am she's back.

Kat claws her fingernails across my shoulders and moans, "Oh, God, when you go slow like that, it's like the sweetest torture."

Looking down at her, I tilt my hips forward to fill her again. "I want to take my time and fuck you slowly so you can never leave this bed," I groan as I slide my cock back inside her.

"I don't care how you do it. Fast, slow, just don't stop. Don't stop," Kat begs.

She doesn't have to worry. I don't want to stop. I

want to give her all of me and take all of her for myself.

Her body squeezes my cock every time I retreat from her, as if her body doesn't want to lose that feeling our bodies are creating. I know how she feels. When I leave her, all I can think of is returning to the warmth of her perfect cunt.

I bury myself inside her one last time, and her thighs close around my waist. Trembling against my sides, she comes as she kisses me, and I know for sure I've found what I wasn't even sure I believed existed.

Until Kat.

After a few minutes of silence where the only sound in the bedroom is our breathing, I ease out of her and lie on the bed. She turns to face me and when I turn my head, I see her smiling.

"What's that for?"

"Uh, great sex makes me smile?" she answers with a giggle.

"Well, then I expect you to be happy from this point on because of all the things I can deliver in this world, great sex is at the top of the list."

That gets me an eye roll. Resting her chin on my chest, she says, "You know, that coming from most men would sound like the biggest ego trip I've ever heard."

Curious if we're about to have a fight right after an incredible round of sex, I lift my arms behind my head and stare down at her. "Oh yeah?"

She doesn't back down, clearly wanting to make a point. "Yeah."

"And with me?" I ask, sensing I may not like her answer.

With a tiny smile I know she's trying to temper, she says, "Not so much, strangely enough. Maybe it's because I'm crazy about you, but you never sound like an egomaniac when you say things like that."

"That's because I can deliver the goods. I told you I'm good at two things: food and fucking."

"And everything else is a crapshoot," she says, repeating my own words I said to her the first time we slept together.

Lowering my arms, I pull her to me and kiss her mouth. "Maybe not everything. I might be getting good at this being a one-woman man thing."

"Oh yeah? Who told you that?" she asks with a sharpness in her tone I know is more of her acting like she did on the reality show.

"Nobody. Just a feeling I'm getting."

"Well, if I'm being truthful, you are pretty good at that. And making up when you hurt someone. Along with sex and food."

"Good. I like that."

Kat narrows her eyes to slits and stares down at me. "But you can't rest on your laurels with being a boyfriend. It's like food and sex. You have to make sure you stay on the top of your game."

Her use of that word makes me realize neither one

of us has ever said it before. Boyfriend. I'm someone's boyfriend. I've never been anyone's boyfriend.

Maybe I'll be good at that too.

"I'll do my best," I say with a laugh.

With a sigh, Kat lowers her head to my chest and presses her cheek to the spot above my heart. "I know you will."

And with that, she drifts off to sleep as I enjoy the reality of being the man who's crazy about her. She was a stranger to me and then an enemy before she became someone so important to me that I couldn't just let her disappear from my life.

So this is what it's like to finally be in love.

CHAPTER SIXTEEN

lex

A KNOCK ON MY DOOR ROUSES ME FROM MY daydreams about what Kat and I will do tonight. She's only been gone for a few minutes, so maybe she came back instead of going to her apartment.

I hurry to the door, thrilled to spend a little more time with her before I have to go to the studio in a couple hours. I'll make her breakfast and feed her in bed. Crepes with bourbon instead of the brandy the recipe calls for. I think I have apricot preserves that will go nicely with them.

By the time I get to the door, I've got the entire breakfast menu planned out in my head. She'll be so surprised, but that's a good thing. I can't wait to see the look on her face.

I fling open the door and see not Kat but my friend Evan. "Hey! I wasn't expecting to see you standing in my hallway. What's up?"

He waves a piece of paper in front of my face and walks past me into my apartment. "I've got the results of the tests you wanted me to run. I was hoping you'd be up and not laying around in bed with some woman at this hour."

As I follow him down the hallway to the living room, I chuckle. "If you got here a little while ago, that's exactly what I was doing."

Evan looks back at me and smirks. "Good old Alex. You never change."

That's not true anymore, but I don't want to explain how Kat has made such a difference now that she's the only woman in my life. For the time being, I want to keep who we are to one another to ourselves.

"Yeah, well you know how it is. So what did you find out? Was there anything in the water?"

His eyes open wide as he shakes his head. "Whoever you were with definitely tried to drug you. Roofies, just as you suspected. I swear I'll never in my life understand why women think they need to give us that shit to get us to fuck them. Just ask. Nine times out of ten, most guys will jump at the chance to get laid."

I take the report when he hands it to me and

glance at the results. So Emma did slip something into my drink. Or maybe it was Randy working with her to fuck me up. I don't care about the specific details. All I care about is telling Maria and Shane and seeing what they do with this information.

Looking up from the paper, I shrug. "As if guys are that difficult to get into bed. I wouldn't have slept with this one, though, so maybe she figured that out."

"Not good looking enough?" Evan asks, knowing me for long enough that his guess is a good one.

At least for who I used to be.

I shake my head. "No, she was hot. A little too eager, but still hot. I just didn't want to sleep with her. Call it a vibe or intuition. My gut said don't get involved with this one, and I guess it was right, huh?" I say as I hold the paper up between us.

"I guess so."

"You want to know what the ballsy thing about what she did was?" I ask, still in disbelief that Emma drugged my drink at my own restaurant. "She did it at CK. Now that's balls the size of Texas."

My friend's mouth drops open in shock before he lets out a surprised laugh. "Get the fuck out of here! She came to your playground and thought she should slip you some shit in your drink right under your father and uncle's noses? This woman has a set on her, no doubt."

"And I'll go you one better. I don't think this is her first time putting something in someone's food or drink. I think she slipped something into a dish a friend of mine on the show made that sent another contestant to the hospital. The unlucky guy had to get his stomach pumped because she poisoned him."

That makes his eyes grow even wider. "Seriously? Is she one of the contestants on that reality show? You better watch out if she is. Bitch has serial killer tendencies."

I nod my agreement with that statement. "No kidding. They wanted me to have some romantic storyline with her. I'm going to show the producers this report and tell them they can go fuck themselves if they think I'm going to pretend to like this woman."

"Fuck that! A man would have to make sure to sleep with one eye open at all times with someone like that," he says with a laugh. "She better be one fantastic lay if she's going to be that much trouble."

"Yeah, I'm not thinking she's good enough for me to take that chance. Sex isn't worth risking my life for, that's for sure. I'd rather be celibate if that's the case."

Evan checks his watch for the time and then slaps me on the shoulder. "You? Celibate? Now I've heard it all. The next thing you'll be telling me is you're settling down with one woman. I have to get to the lab, but call me after you're done with this show and we'll go out for drinks. It's been a while since I got to witness Alex March in action."

I don't bother mentioning those nights won't be happening anymore for me. I'll handle that when we hang out. For now, I just smile and act like I'm the same person I've always been.

Even though I'm not, all because of Kat.

"Thanks for this," I say as I follow him to the door. "Now to see what the producers of the show do with this information."

He opens my front door and turns to look back at me. "Maybe explain to them that getting drugged by a fellow contestant might mean you need to find a lawyer. I bet they see how bad it is then."

"That might be a good thing to bring up. Thanks, Evan."

Now to see what Maria and Shane have to say about the proof I'm holding in my hand.

I SEE EMMA AS SOON AS I WALK ONTO THE SET, BUT I don't meet her gaze as I make a beeline for where the producers are sitting on the side of the room. On the way here, I decided that if they don't get rid of Emma and invite Kat back, I'll bail on this whole stupid reality show.

It's entirely up to them if I do that.

They're huddled together talking in hushed tones about something when I approach them, and normally, I wouldn't interrupt. What I have to talk to them about is too important to wait, though, so I clear my throat and pause a few seconds before I start in on what I have to say.

"I need to tell you something, and what you do about it is going to affect what I decide about staying on this show."

The two of them turn their heads to look at me, and for a long moment, the three of us just stare at one another. When they finally sit up and shift in their seats to face me, I have the sense they resent my disturbing them.

Too bad. I resent have to run interference through a dinner date because one of their contestants is a goddamned criminal.

"When Emma and I went out to dinner for our date, she tried to drug me. Roofie me, actually. Thankfully, someone gave me a head's up, and I didn't drink any of what she drugged. To be honest, I'm not sure it was only her. I get the feeling your cameraman was in on it too."

Both Shane and Maria stare at me for a long moment, probably trying to process all of that, and then her mouth drops open in shock. His doesn't, though, and I immediately wonder why he's not more surprised by anything I just said.

"That doesn't sound like something she'd do," he says, showing his hand about what he thinks of her. "I'm having a hard time believing any of this."

Although Maria looked upset by my announcement at first, now she shakes her head and agrees with her fellow producer. "That's a very serious charge to make, Alex. I'm not sure what you think we can do without proof. I mean, we can't just go throwing people off the show because someone says they were drugged. We need more than that."

Putting aside her hypocrisy since that's exactly what they did to Kat, I hold up the sheet of paper with the lab report on it and say, "This is a report on something found in my drink at dinner the other night, the one Emma and I went to at CK. Now before you even think of saying that someone at my restaurant slipped Rohypnol into my water, stop yourself. My people wouldn't do that, plus one of the owners tipped me off to my drink being drugged after he saw the stuff actually being put into my glass. I don't know if it was Emma or Randy or the two of them, but they were the only ones at the table when he watched a hand holding a vial of something pour it into my water glass."

Maria holds her hand out to take the lab report, so I give it to her. "It's right there. Roofies in my water. What I want to know is what are you going to do about it? And by the way, this should make you take a much harder look at who actually poisoned that chicken bourguignon because it wasn't Kat."

Now the two of them look stunned. Shane leans over to look at the report as Maria studies it and I wait. Anything less than a full investigation and Emma's speedy removal from this show will mean I leave.

"We're going to have to check into this, Alex. I

hope you understand," Maria says in a shell-shocked voice.

"That's fine. I want a full investigation. You need to know that I won't be doing anything more with either of them. No more pretending to like her for some stupid storyline the audience will love. No more going anywhere off this set with either one of them."

The two producers nod their heads in solemn agreement, clearly shaken by my claim and the proof I have to back it up. "I'll give you a day or so, but if she's not removed from this show by then, I'll leave. You got rid of Kat without a shred of evidence she did anything to that food. I expect whatever investigation you do to be quick and Emma gone. You have proof right in your hand. I'm more than happy to give you Kane Jackson's number. He's the owner who saw it happen at the restaurant."

Shane holds up his hand at my mention of Emma's removal. "Now wait a second. You can't demand a contestant be gone. We need to look into this, and it may take a while."

Taking a step toward them, I say, "Then I'll be speaking to an attorney tomorrow morning. Your choice. You handle this and we move on, or we get lawyers involved. It's up to you."

My threat changes his tone, and he immediately agrees to handling the problem quickly. "Okay, okay. You don't need to do that. We'll handle this. We promise, Alex."

When I walk away, I see Emma eyeing me up while I head toward my area to begin the day. It's her or me. That's all there is to it.

And then when she's gone and everyone knows what she did, I plan on doing everything I can to get Kat back on this show where she belongs.

I WATCH KAT'S FACE AS I TELL HER THE WHOLE story about my date with Emma. Her expression morphs from surprised to horrified by the time I reach the part about the roofies.

"Oh my God! You didn't drink any of the water, did you?"

Shaking my head, I shrug. "No. My uncle saw her or Randy, whoever it was that did it, put the stuff into my glass. Thank God he caught me before I went back to the table because if no one had seen it, I would have been completely at her mercy in the back of that limo."

"That bitch! And here I thought she was a nice person all along."

"Not so nice that she won't use a little drugs to get someone to do what she wants."

Kat gets up from the sofa and looks down at me. "I'm not surprised Maria and Shane weren't all about finding out the truth at first. Look what they did to me. Talk about judge and jury convicting without any proof. They had me off that show so quickly my head was still spinning the next day. I'm going to get another beer. You want one?"

I hold up my half-filled bottle to show her I'm good. "Thanks, but I'm nursing mine because I'm too busy telling my story."

While she's gone to the refrigerator, I say, "I didn't tell you the best part, though. Wait until you hear this."

"What?" she calls out from the kitchen. "Hang on. I'll be right there. Don't say anything until I get back because I want to hear every word."

I can't wait to tell her what I have planned. Finally, I'll get to make up for my mistake.

She walks back into the room and sits down next to me. "I'm not going to lie. I wish they'd find out she tried to drug you and also was the one who put whatever it was in my entrée so I could come back, but I doubt they're going to let me."

"That's what I wanted to tell you. When they find out it really was her, I plan to make sure she goes and you come back. I don't see why they won't invite you to come back on the show. They're going to need someone to fill Emma's spot since they're already down two people."

Kat takes a sip of beer and shakes her head. "That sounds like a lot of confusion, though, doesn't it? One show she's there, and the next she's gone replaced by me? I don't know if the audience will like that."

I lower my head and look at her like she's lost her

mind. "Are you kidding? Drama is the name of the game for these people. They'll love it. They'll probably make you the star of the show. Unjustly accused and then redeemed while the person who tried to ruin you is sent packing? That's ratings gold right there."

That makes her smile, and I love how beautiful she looks right now. She has no idea how incredible she is. I wish she could see what I see when I look at her.

"I think you're starting to think like Maria and Shane, you know that? Ratings gold? That's TV talk," she says, teasing me.

I pull her to me and kiss her softly on the lips. "Then let's hope they see me as one of them and do what I want. Either way, I'll be happy. Either they get rid of her, or I'll go. Their choice. I would like to be able to get you back on the show, though, so I want them to send her packing."

Resting her head on my shoulder, she smiles up at me. "Normally, I'd say my luck isn't good enough to have that happen, but who knows? We're together and I never thought that would happen, so maybe they'll do what you demand. You do have a way of charming people into giving you what you want, Alex March."

"Oh yeah? Exactly how do I do that?" I ask while I slide my hands down her sides to cup her ass.

Snuggling up against my body, she giggles. "Exactly like this."

I nuzzle her neck until I realize what she said. Lifting my head, I say, "I can tell you that I've never kissed Maria or Shane, and I swear I've never grabbed either of their asses."

"Promise?"

God, she's cute when she's like this. I pull her up onto my lap and slide my hand around her neck to bring her mouth to mine. Against her lips, I whisper, "I promise. Now let's see how much I can charm you tonight."

"I'm betting a lot."

"Oh yeah? You're going to make me cocky," I say with a smile.

Kat levels her gaze on me like she can't believe what I just said. "Make you cocky? Baby, you've got cocky down to a science. But don't worry. That's one of my favorite parts about you."

She winks, and all I can think of is how happy this woman makes me. Who would have believed a dedicated single man like myself could end up like this?

CHAPTER SEVENTEEN

I DRAG MYSELF TO THE BATHROOM TO BRUSH MY teeth before it gets too late in the day and I become a veritable slob with stinky breath and dirty teeth for too many hours. I'm like this every time I have to go to work. The hours I spend with Alex are incredible. Like seriously incredible. Like I've never been with anyone who's this good in bed incredible.

But the other hours of my life are filled with dread because I have to go back to that kitchen and deal with Deidre. I'm wondering how long it is before she demotes me to dishwasher since she's such a bitch to me. You'd swear I stole her man or killed her parents or something by how awful she is. I think she stays up late each night devising new ways of torture for me.

My teeth clean and my breath minty fresh, I smile at myself in the mirror. God, I do look good when I'm happy. Too bad fifty percent of my life is full of misery courtesy of my boss.

I should get dressed. I've been lounging around in my yoga pants and a t-shirt since I got home from Alex's. It's just that changing my clothes means my time away from Frederick's is almost over, and I hate that.

My phone rings, tearing me out of the cycle of anxiety I go through every day before my shift starts. Assuming it's Alex, I answer it immediately, but to my surprise, it's not him but Maria.

"Kat, I was wondering if you'd be able to come to the studio right now. Shane and I would like to meet with you."

"About what? You threw me off the show. Remember?"

"Yes, about that. We would really like you to come in. Can you be here as soon as possible?"

Did Alex actually convince them to invite me back? Excitement courses through me, but I don't want to sound desperate, so I keep my voice level as I say, "I have work this afternoon, so I can't be there for long."

Surprisingly, she's fine with that. "That's okay. I

don't think what we have planned will take long. See you in a couple!"

So the producers want to see me. As I slide my phone into my pants pocket, I wonder if they plan to apologize for accusing me of poisoning poor Murphy. That would be nice to hear. Even better would be for them to tell me they want me back on the show.

I guess I'll see what they want when I get to the studio.

MY HEART SLAMS INTO MY CHEST WHEN I PUSH open the door to step onto the set of Chef on Chef again. I've only been gone for a week, but I feel like a stranger here now, especially after being escorted out in shame that day.

With each step, I get more nervous. My palms are so sweaty I have to wipe them on my pants. If I need to shake hands with anyone, they're going to think they're touching a damp fish.

I glance around for any sign of Alex, but no one seems to be in the studio today. Was Maria pulling a prank on me? Why would everyone be gone?

"Hello?" I call out, hoping the next thing that happens isn't someone turning all the lights out. This literally feels like half a dozen horror films I've seen in my life.

"Kat? We're over here!" Maria yells from a door off the set.

Strange. I've never noticed that room before. Was it always there?

Cautiously, I walk in that direction, terrified something bad is about to happen. My gut says this isn't good. I don't know if it's horror film bad, but this feels off.

But when I reach her, Maria is all smiles and wraps her arm around my shoulders to guide me into the room. I see Shane sitting at a table looking just as warm and friendly as his fellow producer. Okay, maybe this won't be bad.

"Thank you for coming in on such short notice. We wanted to talk to you about what happened," he says as I sit down across from him and Maria takes a seat right next to him.

"Okay. I'm not sure what there is to talk about," I say, not sure I want to let them in on the fact that I know all about Emma's attempt at drugging Alex on their date the other night.

Better to let them do all the talking here.

"Well, we thought it would be a good idea to get the truth out once and for all," Maria says in her usual overly chipper way.

"The truth? I didn't poison poor Murphy. I would never do that just like I would never tamper with another chef's knives. I told you all of this that day, but you didn't want to hear it and had me escorted out of the building by security."

As I say that, my gut tells me something is wrong

here. Looking around, I see this room is set up with cameras from every angle. Are they taping me? Why did they want to meet me in here?

"What's going on? You heard all of that already, and you don't seem to be doing much talking, so I'm getting a weird vibe here. Where are all the other contestants?" I ask, my anxiety ratcheting higher notch by notch as the seconds tick by.

Just then, the door opens and Emma walks in. This is wrong. Why is she here if they wanted to talk to me?

I move to get up, but Shane quickly stops me. "Wait. Kat, we know what happened. Emma knows too."

My former friend looks at me and then him with total confusion. "I have no idea what you mean. Why did Randy tell me I needed to come in here to talk to you guys if she's in here?"

"Emma, sit down. We have things to discuss," Maria says in a somber tone that's unlike anything I've ever heard come from her before.

"Things to discuss? Like what? And why is Kat here? You threw her off the show for good reason. She poisoned someone. Why would you have her back here?" Emma says, practically spitting my name from her mouth.

"I didn't poison anyone!" I scream, already tired of whatever's going on here. "You did. Just like you tried to drug Alex on your supposed date the other night.

Oh, yeah. I know all about that. You actually thought you could make him want you if you roofied him? That's so pathetic!"

Rage shoots from her eyes, and I watch her hands tighten into fists at her side. "That's a lie! Now she's here trying to get me thrown off the show too." Turning toward Shane and Maria, she says, "Can't you see what she's doing? She was sleeping with Alex, and she's jealous because he and I went to dinner. She's insane!"

I slam my chair into the table to get everyone's attention. "I am not insane. I never drugged anyone. It was you all along. You pretended to be my friend, but you were out to get me the entire time. You probably did this on the first reality show you were on. They probably kicked you off that one too, didn't they?"

As Emma seethes, Maria says, "We know about everything, Emma. Randy confessed to it all. He told us what you did with Alex's drink, and he told us it was you who came in here with his help that night and put something in Kat's chicken bourguignon. What I'm curious about is why."

Her eyes grow wild, and for a moment, I'm worried I made a mistake pushing that chair away from me. At least it could have been a small buffer to stop her if she decides to attack me, which is exactly what she looks like she wants to do right now.

Thankfully, Shane stands up and says, "It's over, Emma. All we want is to know why. Why make it look like Kat poisoned the food? Clearly, you liked Alex, so why would you want him to be hurt by eating it?"

"I didn't think he'd eat it. I thought she would!" she screams with such venom in her voice that I back up a few steps.

The three of us shake our heads, clearly not understanding Emma's motives. Why does she hate me so much?

"So you wanted to make Kat sick? Why?"

"Because then she'd be off the show! I know who her father is. I bet she gets preferential treatment all the time because she's the daughter of the great Andrew Truesdale. Then I saw how well she and Alex were getting along that day, and I hated that. She knew I liked him, but no. She was over there smiling and laughing, as if she actually liked him after telling me she hated everything about him. So I put the drug into her precious dish and assumed she'd eat it the next day. But then you made us switch and poor Murphy got stuck eating her terrible food."

I listen as she confesses to trying to ruin me and wonder how she could ever think I get anything good because of who my father is. All I've ever gotten for being related to Andrew Truesdale is an inferiority complex and more insecurity than any one person should ever have to carry around.

Shane looks up toward one of the cameras near the ceiling and asks, "Did we get all of that?"

A man's voice from somewhere outside the room

answers, "Yep. Got it all. This is going to be great for the show."

Emma's mouth drops open in shock, and a security guard walks through the door. "The police are waiting outside just as you asked me to do, Miss Sanchez. Miss, you need to come with me."

"What? Are you fucking kidding me? I'm being thrown off the show? No way!" Emma screeches.

"Not only that. You're being arrested for poisoning Murphy and trying to poison Alex," Shane says with a satisfied grin. "Take her away, Mick."

I watch in stunned amazement as she tries to run and then fights the security guard every step of the way, screaming that this isn't fair and she didn't do anything wrong. Never in my wildest dreams did I expect this meeting to go like this.

And to think I thought today was going to be like every other day.

Once security escorts her out of the room and closes the door, Shane and Maria take their seats again and ask me to sit down once more. "We would like to have you back on the show. There are only a few more days of taping, but we've come up with a way to shoot your time so it can be edited in. You're a great chef, Kat, and we wish this never happened. We're sorry."

An apology and an invitation to rejoin the show? I must be living someone else's life because great things like this never happen to me.

Then again, I do have an incredible man in my life

now for the first time in ages, so maybe things are turning around for me.

I can't stop myself from grinning ear to ear when I say, "I'd love to come back. I'm going to be honest, though. I'm with Alex now, and I have no intention of breaking things off with him for anything, including this show. If that isn't okay, then I'll have to decline your offer."

Fraternization with other contestants is against our contracts, but having a man like him is worth a thousand chances at a grand prize of a million dollars. They may not understand, but it doesn't matter.

I know the value of what Alex and I have.

After they mumble a few things to each other, they both turn to me and Maria says, "We're fine with that. So is that a yes to coming back?"

I nod, happy I stood my ground and stood up for what matters. "It's a yes."

"Just so you know, that whole thing with Emma is going to be edited into the show," Shane says with a chuckle.

For a second, I worry that I came off too mean and viewers will see me as a bitch, but you know what? I don't care. Call me a bitch or a shrew or anything else, but I told the truth and showed I wouldn't let anyone run all over me anymore.

I bet my father would be proud.

CHAPTER EIGHTEEN

lex

I LOOK AROUND THE STUDIO AT ALL THE contestants I've spent the last couple weeks with and can't help but think this experience hasn't been all terrible. Yes, Emma poisoned Murphy, but he's okay now and she's been arrested. And yes, she tried to drug me, but Kane made sure that didn't happen.

But the best thing about Chef on Chef was meeting Kat. We had a rough start, but these past few days have been nothing short of perfect. During the day, we act like we're just two people competing for a million-dollar prize, but at night, we make up for all that pretending not to care about one another with hours of fantastic sex, great conversations, and the most fun I've ever had with a woman.

All in all, this reality show has been an experience I'll never forget.

Shane walks out to the middle of the set and waves his hands to get everyone's attention. "Okay, it's our last day together, and Maria and I have made it an easy one. We want to thank you for a great show! It's been exciting, hasn't it?"

I glance over at Kat a few stations away, and she gives me a look that says she might call all that happened something other than exciting. I wink at her, hoping she remembers what I said we'd do tonight to celebrate finally being done with Chef on Chef. I've got a surprise for her too, and I can't wait to give it to her.

"Okay, okay. It has been a wild ride at times, but I think we can all honestly say it's been memorable," Shane says with a chuckle. "Today, we're going to end our time together with interviews, so be ready when we yell your name. Alex, you're up first!"

As I walk over to where Maria and Shane wait, I give Kat a tiny smile. We're supposed to pretend we aren't actually dating, but since the show is over, I figure it couldn't hurt. So what if people know?

Taking my seat in front of the camera, I look around this area of the set for the final time. When I had my first interview, I had no idea what this experience would be like. That day, Kat and I got into it, and I had a feeling I was going to hate everything about doing this show.

It's amazing how things change.

"So Alex, tell us about how working on your first reality show has been?" Maria asks. "Did you have a good time?"

Unsure if I should mention anything about the criminal acts Emma carried out, I stick to the positives I have about the show. "You know, I didn't expect this to be life changing for me, but it turns out it was. I came to this with a passion for cooking and loving being a chef, but I found something more to care about, and for that, I'll always remember Chef on Chef as a good thing."

Shane nods as I give my answer, obviously pleased, and when I finish, he asks, "Did you have fun? We always hope that contestants have a good time on all of our shows."

I can't mention falling for Kat or anything about how great things are with her, but I did have a good time in the end. "I always find a good time in everything I do, so I definitely can say I had fun with this. You have to make the best of what you're given, and at times, that was absolutely where I was on this show, but all in all, I think I can say I had a good time."

Ten minutes later after half a dozen more questions about the people I worked with, what I learned about being a chef, and what I plan to do if I win the million dollars, my interview is over. Maria and Shane thank me for my honesty, although I have a feeling they would have appreciated me more if I never told them the truth about what happened with Emma at CK. That's on them. I walk away from all of this with a clear conscience.

I watch a few of the other contestants give their interviews, and then it's time for Kat's. As she walks by, I whisper, "Good luck," and get a faint smile in return. She's nervous, but she shouldn't be. She proved herself to everyone here, especially Maria and Shane. She should be nothing but proud of her time on Chef on Chef.

"Kat, it's been pretty wild, hasn't it?" Shane says, giving everyone a laugh with the understatement of the entire show.

She takes a deep breath and lets it out in a rush before answering, "It has been wild, but it's also been a great experience for me, and for that, I want to thank you and Maria."

The entire studio falls silent at her response, and I sense all our fellow contestants and even the producers have a newfound respect for her. I like that for Kat. She deserved better than she got for most of the show, but she showed them she was tough. She says that makes her a bitch. I say it makes her a strong woman.

And there's nothing sexier in my mind than a woman who knows her own power.

"What did you learn from being on Chef on Chef, Kat?" Maria asks.

Straightening her back, she sits tall on that purgatorial wooden stool and answers, "I learned that I shouldn't be afraid to be who I am. Not everyone is going to like me, but that's okay. I like me. In fact, I like me a lot, and I'm proud of what I did on this show."

I can't help but smile as every answer she gives gets better and better. By the time she's finished, I'm sure she's going to be the winner. That will make my surprise less than I hoped it would be, but her having that money to open her own restaurant will be all I could wish for her.

When she walks up to me after her interview is over and the next one has begun, she whispers, "I did okay, didn't I? I wasn't too cocky, was I?"

"You did great. Cocky or not, I think you're going to win this."

Kat shakes her head. "I can't believe that. I wasn't even here for a bunch of days. I bet it'll be you. They love you. The camera loves you, and I bet the audience is going to be crazy about you."

With a smile, I whisper, "Just as long as a certain chef is crazy about me. That's all I care about."

Before she walks away, she leans in and says in a low voice, "She is."

~

KAT PEEKS AROUND ME AT THE DINNER I'M MAKING her to celebrate the end of our time on Chef on Chef and my big surprise for her. "That smells incredible! You really should have won, you know. That lamb dish you made for the finale yesterday was so good I thought Maria was going to ask to have your babies."

I shake my head and laugh at the way she describes what was actually more like Maria merely enjoying some good lamb. "I'm still blown away that Angus won. Not that his affinity for haggis wasn't interesting, but I didn't see him as the guy who was going to walk away with the million bucks. And how about him deciding to open an Asian fusion restaurant? Angus the Asian fusion lover. Go figure."

She wraps her arms around my waist and presses her cheek to my back. "I did not see that coming. It's okay, though. I think you and I can say we won more, even if we didn't get the grand prize."

Glancing back at her, I nod. "No doubt. Are you ready for the world's best meatloaf?"

"I am," she says with a giggle before releasing her hold on me. "I'll get the plates. You work your magic."

"I'm not sure what I can do with a lowly meatloaf, but I'll try. Maybe a sprig of parsley will make it look pretty."

KAT SNUGGLES AGAINST MY SIDE, THE TWO OF US stuffed from eating too much meatloaf. Who knew something so run-of-the-mill could be so delicious? See, this is why she's talented, even though she doesn't think she is.

"I'm forever adding bacon and cheddar cheese to meatloaf from now on," I say while I run my fingertip up and down her arm.

"You've never had it like that? I figured everyone at least put cheese in their meatloaf," Kat says with a chuckle.

"Nope. In fact, when you mentioned making meatloaf, I cringed a little because I've always hated it."

She sits up and stares at me in disbelief. "Why didn't you tell me? We could have made something else, something at least that you knew you liked."

"Because I trusted you. You're a talented chef, Kat. I knew you wouldn't suggest it if you didn't think it was good, and you were right. I think the weight I put on from that dinner says so too," I say with a smile.

Leaning in, she kisses me sweetly. "Thank you for believing in me. I don't think I do that enough, but you're so confident that when you say you trust me, it means a lot to me, Alex."

"I do believe in you. You're a great chef. In fact, I think you'd be an even better chef if you had a better place to work."

I've been waiting for hours to spring this on her. Actually, it's been days since I talked to my father and

Kane about my idea, and all that time, I've been dying to tell her.

"Maybe," she says, shrugging like it's not a big deal that she hates her job.

But it is, and I want to do something about that.

"Kat, I want to talk to you about work. I want you to come to CK as a sous chef."

Her green eyes open wide, followed by her mouth dropping open in shock. "What? You want me to work for you?"

"With me," I say with a smile. "We'd work together at a place where you could be as great as you want to be. As great as I think you can be in a kitchen. You'd be second chef in title only, and when my father and uncle retire and I get the restaurant, I'll want you to be head chef. What do you say?"

As I expected, her emotions get the best of her, and she begins to tear up. Smiling, though, she nods and gives me my answer. "Yes! Oh, my God, yes! I would love to come work with you at CK. It's like a dream come true!"

She throws her arms around my neck and sobs, "Thank you for believing in me. You have no idea how much this means to me."

I close my eyes and revel in the feel of her against my body. She belongs with me, and I belong with her. That's what I believe in more than anything.

And then, for the first time in my life, those three little words I've never said to any woman I've ever dated fill every inch of my brain until I can't think of anything but saying them. It's probably too soon and she might not say them back, but I can't do anything other than tell her how I feel.

"I love you, Kat."

I'd always wondered if I'd ever say that to someone. The words come out like they're the most natural thing in the world for me to say right now, and when I finish speaking, I let out a sigh, as if I've waited my entire life to feel this way.

Kat stills in my arms, and then after a few seconds, she sits back to look at me. I see in her expression she's surprised. "You love me?"

"Yeah. Believe me, I'm a little shocked too. Not that I love you, but that I finally said those words. I've never told any woman I loved her until you."

"You've never said I love you to anyone before me?" she asks with shock in her voice and her expression.

I shake my head. "Nope. Never. Then when you said yes to coming to work at CK, those words were all I could think of. I love you, Kat. For all the madness you bring to my life and all the things we love to do together, I love you. Damn, now that I finally said them I can't seem to stop."

She cradles my face in her hands and kisses me long and slow before pulling away to give me a gentle smile. "I love you, too, Alex. I have said those words before, and I swore I'd never say them again, but being with you makes me happier than I've ever been in my life. I can't believe I ever thought I hated you. What was I thinking?"

"I'm just glad you don't anymore."

Wrapping her arms around me again, she hugs me tightly as she kisses my neck. "I must have been crazy."

"Tonight's been a good night. Great meatloaf, you agreeing to come work at CK, and we love each other."

Giggling, she leans back and taps me on the tip of my nose. "You are very cute sometimes. No wonder everyone's crazy about you."

"The only one I care about being crazy about me is you, Kat."

"Don't worry. I am."

We started out as enemies, and now we're in love. Maybe that reality show was good after all.

CHAPTER NINETEEN

at

NEVER BEFORE HAVE I LOOKED FORWARD TO GOING into work like I do today. This time, I'm not walking into the kitchen at Frederick's and cringing as I wait for Deidre to lower the boom on me. Those days are over now that I get to go work at CK with Alex.

After I thanked him for my new job with great sex, I told him every moment of what I plan to do when I tell that nasty harpy I'm leaving. She can have her two weeks, but I'm already gone from this place, so nothing she can do will upset me ever again.

She's standing near the grill hovering over one of the chefs and barking out orders at him when I enter the kitchen. God, she's rotten! It would serve her right if every one of us left to work at other restaurants. I swear this woman thinks she's Gordon Ramsay.

"Alfredo, do you understand the idea of searing to make grill marks, or don't they teach that to cooks anymore?" she snaps as he cowers next to her.

"Deidre, I need to speak to you," I say loudly, taking the attention away from her outburst attacking him.

"I'm busy. Later," she says without even turning around to acknowledge I'm there.

At this point, I'd usually just skulk away like some child who's just been chastised, but not today. Kat Truesdale is not going to wait until it's more convenient for the person who's made her life a living hell. That's the old me. New me demands a little more respect.

"No. Now," I say even more loudly.

Everything in the kitchen seems to stop. No chefs move, although a couple glance over at me and give me tiny smiles. They know what it feels like with her. I bet they wish they could do what I'm doing right now. I hope they can someday because it feels great.

Deidre spins around and marches over to me, stopping just before she runs me over. Her hands on her hips, she says, "I'm busy, Katerina. You should be too since your shift starts in five minutes, so go get dressed and get back here to start working."

"I need to speak to you about something. Can we go into the office?"

"No. Whatever you have to say, you can say right here."

Fine. We'll have this talk right in the middle of the kitchen. Seems only right that everyone will see me give my notice since they've watched her give me every reason in the book to leave for months on end.

"I'm giving you my two weeks' notice. I've gotten another job. I'm leaving."

No words have ever made me feel freer than those. I've dreamed of saying them for so long I sometimes wondered if they'd ever become reality, but now that I'm standing in front of the woman who's made me hate my job on so many days and the words are actually out now, it's the best feeling in the world.

"What do you mean? What other restaurant would hire you? You're a salad prep," she says with an edge in her voice that shows just how little she thinks of me.

But I'm not going to let her bring me down. Not today. Not ever again.

"I am a chef and a damn good one at that. I've been a chef here for over two years, and I did a good job despite having no support from my head chef. It's none of your concern what restaurant would want me because they do, so this is your two weeks' notice."

She seethes at my confidence, shaking her head in disgust. "Don't bother. I can replace you at salad in less than a day. You can turn in everything that belongs to the restaurant right now."

For a moment, I'm stunned by her words, but that

doesn't last for long. Being given my freedom two weeks early has made this day even better.

Spinning on my heels, I yell back as I walk out through the kitchen door, "Good luck everyone! Except you, Deidre. I hope you get what you deserve."

My hands are shaking, and I feel like I might burst into tears as I march out of the restaurant into the midday sun. I'm free. No waiting fourteen days to start my new job. No dealing with her insults and haranguing.

I'm free!

I see Heidi as I'm walking to my car and tell her the great news. She throws her arms around me and says, "You deserve so much better than she ever gave you. Good luck, Kat! I know you're going to be great."

"Thanks. Come see me sometime at my new restaurant. I'll make you something incredible, okay?"

As she heads into the building, she calls back, "I'm going to hold you to that. Don't be surprised when I show up at CK one night looking great and wanting to see you."

I hope she does.

ALEX IS WAITING FOR ME OUTSIDE OF CK WHEN I arrive. After I tell him all the wonderful details about how I told Deidre I was giving her my notice and stood my ground, even when she insulted me and said

I was so easily replaced that I could leave today, I take a deep breath and look at the front of my new workplace.

"I can't believe I'm going to be a chef here. I think it's finally sunk in, and now I'm a little nervous. Who do I have to meet today?"

"My father and my uncle. You've already met my father. Remember that night we were in his office?"

I cringe at that memory. "Oh, God. He must think I'm a crazy person. I was so mean to you that night."

Alex takes hold of my hand and brings it to his mouth to kiss my knuckles. "All water under the bridge, and don't worry about what he thinks. He was the one who called me that night to tell me you and your parents were here."

"And he's okay with us being together while we're both working here? Most places don't allow fraternization."

A sexy smile lifts the corners of his beautiful mouth. "Sometimes there are benefits to being the owner's son. Now as for Kane, he looks just like my father, but he usually has a serious look on his face. He's sort of the grumpy owner."

"Okay. Got it."

Then it dawns on me I don't remember his father's name. "Kane is the uncle, but what's your father's name?"

As Alex begins to walk me into the building, he says, "Cassian. There's another brother too, but he doesn't have anything to do with this business. He's the one who owns Club X."

"Oh, the one Sadie liked who looks like you. Okay. Are there only three brothers?"

He stops for a moment and smiles. "Yes and no, but that's for another time. Right now, just remember Cassian March is my father and Kane Jackson is my uncle."

I feel my palms begin to get sweaty when we walk into the dining room. "I'm glad you told me their last names," I whisper. "I would have made a mistake and called him Kane March. Not exactly the best way to start out at a new job."

Alex looks at me and smiles. "You're going to be fine. I've told them both about how great a chef you are, and this is just a formality. You already have the job. You're sleeping with the head chef."

I throw him a dirty look for that crack. "Stop it! I want them to like me, not let me work here because we're together. No more talking about us sleeping together as long as we're in this building. Got it?"

"Spoken like a true boss. You're going to be a great head chef once I get to be owner of this place."

When I see his father and uncle standing near the door to the kitchen, I grip Alex's hand nervously. He gives me a squeeze in return as if to say, "You're going to be great. Believe in yourself."

I take one more deep breath and then make sure I'm smiling as he introduces me to both men. They're very polite and professional, and I instantly feel welcome, something I never felt at my last job.

"It's good to have you here, Katerina," Cassian says as Kane walks away. "Alex has raved about your work."

"Thank you. I'm thrilled to be working here. But please call me Kat."

"Well, Kat, I know Alex can't wait to show off his kitchen, so I'll let you two get to it. Come see me or Kane when you're done getting your bearings and we can get all the necessary paperwork completed. You know where our office is. It's the one you were in the other night with Alex."

I feel my face heat up, probably turning bright red from embarrassment. "Okay, thanks."

When he leaves, Alex says, "See? That wasn't too bad."

"He mentioned me being in his office the other day. God, he probably thinks I'm such a bitch because we were fighting."

But that doesn't faze Alex. "Don't worry. He knows I had it coming. I fucked up. But he's the one who made sure to get me here to see you and your parents that night, so he can't think too badly of you. Now let me take you to see the kitchen."

When he says that, his eyes light up like a kid in a candy store. I've seen kitchens before, but maybe this one is different.

And then I walk into the kitchen at CK and it's like

entering a world I've only imagined before. Everything is brand new. The stainless-steel shines so I can see my reflection. This is nothing like any kitchen I've ever been in before. This is even more impressive than the kitchens my father has worked in.

I stop dead in front of the ovens and look around, swiveling my head to see everything surrounding me. "This is incredible, Alex. Was it like this when you walked in, or did you make it look like this?"

He puffs out his chest and begins to point out the parts of the kitchen he changed when he became head chef. "I told my father and uncle if they wanted this restaurant to be the best, they needed to invest in a top rate kitchen. So they gave me carte blanche and I went to town. Nearly every piece of equipment in here I chose. So welcome to your new workplace. What do you think?"

"I know many people wouldn't get this, but you will. This kitchen makes me want to cry it's so beautiful. I can't imagine ever being unhappy cooking in here."

"Good. Well, that's the tour. People are going to be coming in for work, so we can stay, and I can introduce you, or we can go and I'll do that at another time. It's up to you."

Suddenly, the fear that everyone is going to think I got this job because of him comes over me. "I'm not sure. I don't want to start out on the wrong foot with anyone. Do you think they're going to hold it against me because we're together and I'm working here now?"

He smiles and shakes his head. "That's not how things are here at CK. This is a family business, and we're all like family here. They're going to love working with you just like I do. Don't worry."

For the first time, I feel like I've finally come to a place where I can be the chef I always wanted to be. To find a family too is almost too much to ask.

"Okay. Then I'll meet everyone on my first shift."

"Sounds good. Welcome to CK, Kat."

A gorgeous boyfriend who loves me and a great new job at the best restaurant in town. If I'm dreaming, I hope I never wake up.

CHAPTER TWENTY

lex

Four months later

Kat fusses with her hair for what feels like the tenth time this morning, hogging the bathroom mirror as she stresses out about what she says is the frizzy mess on the top of her head. It looks fine to me, pretty much like it always does. Dark hair that comes to the middle of her back and feels good when I run my fingers through it.

"It looks like I have a brown haystack on my head! I can't go looking like this!" she cries as she wets her palms yet again.

"I'm not a hair expert, but if humidity makes it frizzy, then won't water make that worse?" I ask, instantly realizing by the look of horror on her face that I've made a terrible mistake.

"So it is frizzy! Oh, God. I'm going to look like a trainwreck, and I really wanted to look good to meet your grandmother for the first time."

She starts to run her hands over her hair again, so I turn her around and take them in mine, stopping her insanity for a few moments. Bringing them to my lips, I kiss her still damp fingertips.

"It's not frizzy. It looks great, just like you always do. And don't worry about meeting my grandmother. I'm the favorite grandson, so you're in."

Kat frowns at my attempt to help. "My hair is a disaster area today, and you being the favorite isn't as good as you think. That means she's probably going to notice every bad thing about me because she likes you best."

I hadn't thought of that, but she's wrong. Alexandria March is going to love her just like I do. "It's going to be fine. My grandmother is going to be crazy about you. She's heard all about you for months. Trust me. Everyone in my family considers it major news that I've settled down with you, so we've been the talk of the entire March and Jackson clan through the last three family events."

Hanging her head, Kat quietly says, "She isn't thinking I was avoiding meeting her those times, is she? I couldn't help it. The first one felt like we weren't dating long enough, and then the last two were because my parents were moving down here and my mother wanted my help those days."

I tilt her chin up so she has to look at me when I try to reassure her. "Nobody thought you were avoiding anything. I told them to mind their own business."

Kat's eyes grow huge. "You told the matriarch of your family to mind her own business? Explain to me again how you're the favorite?"

With a smile, I say, "I'm her namesake. Alexandria and Alexander. From the moment I was born, I was the favorite. She and I are a lot alike too, so that's how I know she's going to love you just like I do, Kat. So don't worry about your hair or anything else. You're a shoo-in today. You've met mostly everyone else, so now it's just her."

She takes a deep breath in and lets it out slowly. "Okay, remind me again who everyone is. I may have met them, but it's hard to keep all of you straight. You're so lucky that you only have to remember my parents' names since I'm an only child."

I can't help but laugh at that. We are a big, crazy group, and I imagine it's hard to keep who's who straight. "Okay. You know my mother and father, Olivia and Cassian. You've met my brother and Savannah that one time. If you aren't sure who he is, look for the guy who looks just like my father with the dark hair and blue eyes."

"But Kane has dark hair and blue eyes too. Jesus, that's confusing."

"I know, but it's the best way to think of it with my brother."

Kat nods and repeats what I said. "Okay. Cash the brother with the blue eyes and dark hair looks like Cassian the father. I'd know Savannah anywhere with that gorgeous light brown hair. She's someone I'd remember anytime."

"Good. Now Kane you know, and I think you've met his wife Abbi, right? Pale blond with big blue eyes?"

"Yes, I've met her. She's so beautiful too. God, her hair always looks so great every time I've seen her at the restaurant."

"Okay. Only one of their kids will be there today because Annalea is still in Australia and Wilder is off in Mexico probably getting thrown into a Mexican jail."

A look of horror settles into Kat's features. "That's a nice thing to say."

"Trust me. If you knew Wilder, you'd agree. Now Liam also has dark hair and blue eyes like my father and Cash, but he's bigger like his father."

Her frustration bubbles over as she tries to remember who everyone is. "Your family is so hard to keep straight. So Liam, Cash, Kane, and Cassian are all dark haired with blue eyes? God, I hope I don't get anyone confused."

I kiss her forehead and smile. "You won't, and if you do, it's not that big a deal. Now Liam will be there with Mia. She's the singer."

"Oh, I'll be able to pick her out too. Good!"

"Okay. Now you know Cade and Hailey because we've been out with them a bunch of times. She's the baker, and he's the guy you met that first night at Club X."

A look of recognition fills her eyes. "Oh, yeah! I know them, and I remember his father, the one who owns Club X. They look like you. Got it. Stefan has a wife, right?"

I nod. "Shay. She might not be there today, but if she is, she's got dark hair too. The only ones who don't have dark hair are my mother and Abbi and my grandmother, of course. You'll know her by the white hair."

Biting her lip, Kat looks scared. "God, I hope she likes me. I don't want to mess this up, Alex."

She really seems terrified about all of this, so I take her in my arms there in the bathroom with her damp hair and needless concern and hold her to me. "You've got this. It's just a bunch of people I'm related to. I know it seems overwhelming, but they're going to love you like I do. Trust me."

Leaning back, she looks up at me with eyes full of worry. "I hope so."

• • •

When we pull up to my grandmother's house, the entire family is waiting on the front porch just to make things extra stressful. Kat turns to look at me, and I see the fear in her eyes as they all stare at the car and us.

"They're doing this to bust my ass because this is the first time I'm bringing someone to one of these things. Don't worry, okay?"

With a heavy sigh, she nods. "Okay. Let's do this giant family thing."

"I'll try to stick close by you so you don't get trapped with any one of them. Oh, and be prepared for pictures from when I was little. They did that to Liam when he first brought Mia here, so I'm expecting my mother and grandmother to break out the family photos."

"That could be fun. Were you a cute little boy?" she asks with a chuckle.

"Of course," I joke. "Let's do this!"

We get out of the car and begin walking up toward the porch where everyone waits, and the ball busting starts from Cade, of course. "Here's the man of the hour, Mr. Eye Candy I'm Going To Be Single Forever," he says just before we hit the steps. "Is that a woman you've brought to one of our fine March and Jackson parties? Did you warn her that we would be busting your ass all day today?"

I would love to tell Cade to fuck off, but my grandmother is standing right next to him, so I roll my eyes at his ball busting. "Everyone, you know Kat. Kat, this is the March and Jackson clan."

Cade begins teasing me again, but he's drowned out by everyone welcoming Kat to the party, thankfully. I follow her up onto the porch and watch the crowd swallow her up as my grandmother pulls me off to the side.

Kat gives me a worried look as she's swept into the house by my mother and Abbi to get a drink. My grandmother walks me over to the other side of the porch as everyone files inside, leaving us alone.

"So my Alex finally has a girl he likes enough to bring to one of our get-togethers. You look happy. Is this the one you were so down about that one day when we talked up in the bedroom you and Cade used to sleep in when you stayed here as little boys?" she asks, clearly wanting to know more about Kat.

I nod, happy to tell her all about the woman I love. "Yeah, that was Kat. I took your advice, and she forgave me. Since then, we've been inseparable, so I figured it was time for you to meet her."

My grandmother's eyes get wide, and she asks, "Does that mean this is the one?"

With a shrug, I answer, "I don't know if we're there yet, but you shouldn't be surprised if we announce something someday."

"Someday like today?" she asks with more than a hint of hope in her voice.

Shaking my head, I laugh at her eagerness. "No,

not today. Kat's nervous about meeting you, so take it easy on her, okay? She's afraid she's going to mess this up and you won't like her."

"Did you tell her that all that matters is how you feel, not how some old woman feels?"

"You know it means a lot what you think, Grandma. You're the head of this family. That's important. I'm crazy about her, though. She's all I've ever wanted."

My grandmother pinches my cheek like she used to when I was little. With a smile, she says, "The last one to settle down. I always knew it would take you longer because you were blessed with so much from the very beginning. If you like her, I like her."

"I love her, Grandma."

I watch as her brown eyes fill with tears. "Oh, that means it's really happened. Good. Let's go in so I can meet the woman who stole my favorite grandson's heart."

As I follow her inside, I say, "You know, every one of us thinks we're your favorite. Do you tell them all the same thing you tell me?"

Glancing back at me, she smiles and gives me a wink. "Yes, but you're my namesake, so you're really the favorite."

Just as I thought.

. . .

THE DAY GOES SMOOTHLY WITH ONLY A FEW moments of ball busting by my brother and cousins for my former stance on forever remaining single, but I notice my grandmother doesn't say much to Kat. Is it possible she doesn't like her?

While I head to the kitchen, I see her finally pull Kat aside in the living room. Curious to know what she's saying, I quickly pour us a couple glasses of iced tea and sneak over to the corner of the room to listen to their conversation.

"I just wanted to tell you it's so wonderful to have you here today, Kat. Alex is my favorite grandson, although don't tell the others because I tell them they are too but he really is, so I always wanted to see him happy."

The smile on Kat's face makes my heart swell and tells me she isn't as nervous as I worried she would be. "Thank you so much for having me. I'm crazy about Alex, and all I want is to see him as happy as he makes me."

My grandmother does that thing where she takes a person's hands in hers and gives Kat a big smile I know is genuine. "My son raves about your abilities as a chef, and I know Olivia is a big fan of yours too, so I'm glad to finally get the chance to finally meet the famous Kat."

"Oh, I don't know if I'm famous. I'm more like just Kat."

"Don't kid yourself. You've caused quite a stir in

this family. Alex swore he was going to be single forever, so you did something pretty incredible. I've watched you two all day, and it's clear to me you're happy, and that makes me happier than I can say."

"Thank you. I was so worried coming here today that I'd mess up someone's name or you wouldn't like me. Thank you for making me feel so welcome with all of you."

In her usual sweet way, Alexandria March opens her arms and gives Kat a big hug. From my vantage point, I see relief wash over her face, and I know she's one of us now.

Katerina March. That has a nice ring to it.

CADE GRABS ME AND HANDS ME A BEER BEFORE pulling me toward the stairs leading down to the beach. "While the girls are all inside, let's go have a beer like old times."

I look in through the kitchen door and see Kat with Savannah, Mia, and Hailey looking at pictures with my grandmother and mother. At least they never disappoint.

"Don't worry. You always look good, so it's not like there's anything they're going to show her that will make her run for the hills," he jokes.

Cash and Liam are already relaxing on the sand, so the two of us join them as the sun begins to set in the distance, giving the water an orange hue that never fails to make me love this place. All my life, the best times were here, and today is no exception.

"Coming to hide out from whatever Grandma is doing inside?" Liam asks with a chuckle. "Be careful, Alex. They get those old family photos out, and the next thing you know, everyone's talking about when you're having kids. I swear that's why Grandma does it."

"Kat seems to be holding up pretty well, all things considered," Cash says. "We can be more than a little overwhelming."

I can't disagree with that. "She's an only child, so this is like being thrown into the belly of the beast for someone like her."

Cade raises his bottle in the air and says, "Here's to the newest girlfriend having to deal with this family. Thankfully, she's got Hailey, Savannah, and Mia to help her."

All four of us hold our beers up and laugh. "There's safety in numbers," Liam jokes.

We sit there silently for a while before Cade says, "So that's it. There are no more of us to settle down."

I give him a look to say he's wrong, and Liam leans forward to look over at him. "Dude, Wilder hasn't settled down."

That gets him an eye roll from Cade, who still hates the only single March or Jackson man left. "Fine, but out of all of us who have always hung out together, Alex is the last to fall."

Turning his attention to me, he asks with a smile, "How's it feel to admit you were wrong and we were right?"

"Right about what?"

My brother answers for him. "We told you that you wouldn't be single forever, but you refused to believe the almighty Alex March would ever settle down with only one woman."

"We're not married, Cash. We're just happy and having a good time, which is very much me, so not much has changed."

His eyes light up, and he reaches into his pocket to throw a hundred down onto the sand. "That calls for a bet. Who's going to be the first to tie the knot? I say Liam."

Cade and I look at each other like we know it won't be us first. "I think it's going to be you, Cash," I say and Cade seconds that idea. "Yeah, I figured it would be you first too."

We look to our left at Liam, who looks like the cat who just swallowed the canary. Leaning back, he slides his hand into his front pants pocket and pulls out a small black velvet box.

"I think Cash might be the winner, but he had inside information since I showed him the ring earlier."

I elbow my brother for trying to bait us into a bet he already knew the outcome of. "Nice trick, Cash."

Liam opens the box and shows us all a huge

diamond engagement ring. Beaming a smile, he says, "I'm planning to ask her tonight."

"Jesus, what did that run you, man? That had to set you back nearly ten grand!" Cade says as he takes a look at it.

"Let's just say it put a nice dent in my savings."

Behind us, the sound of women coming out of the house makes him hurry to put the ring away, and he says in a low voice as they make their way toward us, "Don't say a word. I want Mia to be surprised."

The three of us swear to keep it a secret, and a few seconds later, our foursome becomes an eightsome when all our girlfriends join us. As we all talk for the next half hour, I watch as my brother and cousins look happier than I've ever seen. It might be because I've come around to accepting that being single wasn't the be all end all. Now that I have Kat, I understand this new kind of happiness.

Whatever it is, it warms my heart to see all four of us with women we love.

One by one, each couple says their good nights and leaves until it's just Kat and me down on that beach. The night sky still shows hints of the warm orange from the sunset, and I'm not sure I've ever seen this place more beautiful.

We stand there as the water laps against our ankles, and I kiss her to silently say thank you for making me the happiest man on earth. She looks up at me and says, "I had a wonderful time today, Alex. Your family is incredible."

Nodding, I have to agree. "They are. We can be a big mess of a group, but when it comes down to it, the March and Jackson clan is okay."

As we watch the final tinges of orange fade away, replaced by the darkness of night, I hold her in my arms and think about Liam getting married. That means kids are next for him.

Kat and I aren't there yet, but maybe someday. Even for the last single guy who never thought he'd settle down, the possibility exists.

Now that I've found my Kat.

Keep reading to find out more about K.M.'s books!

ABOUT THE AUTHOR

K.M. Scott writes contemporary romance stories of sexy, intense, and unforgettable love. A New York Times and USA Today bestselling author, she's been in love with romance since reading her first romance novel in junior high (she was a very curious girl!). Under her Gabrielle Bisset name, she writes paranormal and historical romance. She lives in Pennsylvania with a herd of animals and when she's not writing can be found reading or feeding her TV addiction.

Be sure to visit K.M.'s Facebook page at **https://www.facebook.com/kmscottauthor** for all the latest on her books, along with giveaways and other goodies! And to hear all the news on K.M. Scott books first, sign up for her newsletter today and be sure to visit her website at **http://www.kmscottbooks.com**

BOOKS BY K.M. SCOTT

HEART OF STONE SERIES

Crash Into Me (Heart of Stone #1)

Fall Into Me (Heart of Stone #2)

Give In To Me (Heart of Stone #3)

Heart of Stone Volume One

Ever After (Heart of Stone #4)

A Heart of Stone Christmas (Heart of Stone #5)

Return To Me (Heart of Stone #6)

Forever With Me (Heart of Stone #7)

Heart of Stone Volume Two

Hard As Stone (Heart of Stone #8)

Set In Stone (Heart of Stone #9)

Silent As A Stone (Heart of Stone #10)

Heart of Stone Volume Three

All of Me (Heart of Stone #11)

CLUB X SERIES

Temptation (Club X #1)

Surrender (Club X #2)

Possession (Club X #3)

Satisfaction (Club X #4)

Acceptance (Club X #5)

Complete Club X Series Box Set

NeXt SERIES

Notorious (NeXt #1)

Infamous (NeXt #2)

Ravenous (NeXt #3)

Ambitious (NeXt #4)

Flirtatious (NeXt #5)

Mysterious (NeXt #6)

Sensuous (NeXt #7)

Desirous (NeXt #8)

CORRUPTED LOVE TRILOGY

If I Dream (Corrupted Love #1)

If You Fight (Corrupted Love #2)

If We Fall (Corrupted Love #3)

Corrupted Love Trilogy Box Set

ADDICTED TO YOU SERIES

Crave (Addicted To You #1)

Adore (Addicted To You #2)

Shatter (Addicted To You #3)

Claim (Addicted To You #4)

Addicted To You Series Box Set

PROJECT ARTEMIS SERIES

In The Darkness (Project Artemis #1)

After The Storm (Project Artemis #2)

Behind The Scenes (Project Artemis #3)

Project Artemis Box Set

FINDING THE ONE SERIES

Hard Work (Finding The One #1)

Big Love (Finding The One #2)

DIRTY BOSS SERIES

Sweet Things (Dirty Boss #1)

Private Secretary (Dirty Boss #2)

Play Date (Dirty Boss #3)

Dirty Boss Volume One

K.M.'S BOOKS ARE IN AUDIOBOOK TOO!

BOOKS BY K.M. SCOTT WRITING AS GABRIELLE BISSET

SONS OF NAVARUS SERIES

Vampire Dreams Revamped (A Sons of Navarus Prequel)

Blood Avenged (Sons of Navarus #1)

Blood Betrayed (Sons of Navarus #2)

Longing (A Sons of Navarus Short Story)

Blood Spirit (Sons of Navarus #3)

The Deepest Cut (A Sons of Navarus Short Story)

Blood Prophecy (Sons of Navarus #4)

Blood Craving (Sons of Navarus #5)

Blood Eclipse (Sons of Navarus #6)

Blood Ascendant (Sons of Navarus #7)

The Sons of Navarus Box Set #1

The Sons of Navarus Box Set #2

DESTINED ONES DUET

Stolen Destiny (Destined Ones Duet #1)

Destiny Redeemed (Destined Ones Duet #2)

VICTORIAN EROTIC ROMANCES

Love's Master

Masquerade

The Victorian Erotic Romance Trilogy

www.ingramcontent.com/pod-product-compliance
Lightning Source LLC
Chambersburg PA
CBHW031727170626
46808CB00005B/1922

* 9 7 8 1 9 5 5 3 3 5 1 7 1 *